Business Desk Reference

Understanding the Bottom Line

Second Edition

Finance for nonfinancial managers and business owners

CAREER PRESS
180 Fifth Avenue
P.O. Box 34
Hawthorne, NJ 07507
1-800-CAREER-1
201-427-0229 (outside U.S.)
FAX: 201-427-2037

UNDERSTANDING THE BOTTOM LINE (SECOND EDITION)
FINANCE FOR NONFINANCIAL MANAGERS AND BUSINESS OWNERS
ISBN 1-56414-108-X, $8.95
Cover design by Digital Perspectives
Printed in the U.S.A. by Book-mart Press

To order this title by mail, please include price as noted above, $2.50 handling per order, and $1.00 for each book ordered. Send to: Career Press, Inc., 180 Fifth Ave., P.O. Box 34, Hawthorne, NJ 07507

Or call toll-free 1-800-CAREER-1 (Canada: 201-427-0229) to order using VISA or MasterCard, or for further information on books from Career Press.

Library of Congress Cataloging-in-Publication Data

Understanding the bottom line : finance for nonfinancial managers and business owners. -- 2nd ed.
p. cm. -- (Business desk reference)
Prev. ed. cataloged under: Pohlman, Randolph. Understanding the bottom line.
ISBN 1-56414-108-X : $8.95
1. Financial statements--Handbooks, manuals, etc.
2. Corporations--Finance--Handbooks, manuals, etc. I. Pohlman, Randolph. Understanding the bottom line. II. Series.
HF5681.B2P59 1993
658. 15--dc20 93-17887
CIP

Table of Contents

1

UNDERSTANDING AND USING FINANCIAL STATEMENTS

As an effective manager you must have a firm grasp of the basics of financial statements, be able to analyze them and draw conclusions about the firm's performance based on those statements. There are a variety of financial statements that may be used in analyzing a firm's position or performance. These statements include:

Balance Sheet — The balance sheet (also called the statement of financial position) shows all of the items owned or controlled by the firm, the debts owed by the firm and the ownership interest in the firm. The balance sheet must, by definition, balance. Assets must equal liabilities plus stockholders' equity. This is commonly expressed by the accounting equation:

Assets = Liabilities + Stockholders' Equity

Income Statement — The income statement summarizes the firm's operations from its economic activities of buying, producing and selling or providing services for a particular period of time. An income statement includes all of the revenues that the firm generates and all of the expenses that the firm incurs in its operations. It also shows what is often referred to as "the bottom line" or the firm's net income after taxes.

Cash Flow Statement — Unlike the income statement, the cash flow statement shows the cash that came in and the cash that went out of the firm, as well as the firm's net cash inflow or outflow during the reporting period. As you will see in this chapter, the cash flow statement and the income statement are often different because most firms use the accrual accounting method.

Statement of Changes in Retained Earnings — Most firms retain part of their earnings. A statement of changes in retained earnings simply shows what the firm started with in retained earnings, what caused changes in those retained earnings and the new balance. Items that change a company's retained earnings include net income, dividends (distributions) and capital contributions by the owners.

It is important for managers to understand how amounts in each of the financial statements tie together. For example, the ending balance of retained earnings on the statement of changes in retained earnings should agree with the balance of that account on the balance sheet. Another example is that the ending cash balance on the cash flow statement should equal the cash balance on the balance sheet.

Financial statements are used for a wide variety of purposes. If you are considering investing in the firm, you may want to analyze these statements to judge the soundness of the business and whether it would be a good investment for you. You must analyze very carefully the income statement and the balance sheet to determine if the firm is fiscally sound, then combine this knowledge with other information to determine whether the firm has good management and a strong potential. For publicly held companies, this is done by analysts who provide their results to you for a fee.

Individuals or institutions considering making a loan to the firm being analyzed may take a slightly different view from analysts who are considering investing in the firm as owners. Present and prospective creditors are concerned with the amount of debt the firm has, the ability of the firm to pay its debt, the amount of cash it may hold, how readily the firm can turn its assets into cash if it has to liquidate and other standards of lending that may be prevalent in the industry involved.

People interested in taking over a firm also analyze financial statements. This group will be interested in the firm's profit potential, its cash flow potential and what assets may have to be sold to pay for the purchase of the firm while still maintaining the primary operations.

The group who most frequently uses financial statements for analysis includes the firm's managers. Managers have the same concerns as bankers, lending institutions, takeover people and external financial analysts. They also analyze the statements in order to provide better management. They look at the income statement, the balance sheet and other statements — but primarily the income statement — for managerial purposes. The income statement is very much like a report card for the firm. You can look at the report card and get a good idea of how the firm did because it allows you to review all sources of revenue and all expenses to determine how the firm arrived at its net income. You must also carefully examine the balance sheet to see if there are accounts that are too large or too small and, in conjunction with the income statement, whether the assets have been as productive as they could be. How to interpret this information will be covered in depth later in this chapter.

Analyzing financial data is critical for the owners/managers of a new business. Many entrepreneurs do not have the necessary financial background to analyze statements. Many new business owners completely ignore financial data. This does not represent a lack of "business sense," but just a lack of understanding of the necessity of staying well informed about a business' financial matters. For small businesses especially, cash-flow analysis can mean the difference between success and failure.

It is important for you to understand that even though managers, financial analysts, lenders and individuals interested in taking over the business may look at the company from a slightly different angle and have different basic concerns, their fundamental analysis will be similar in many ways. However, any user of financial statements must clearly understand that financial statements are only one portion of the information used to better understand the firm's operations or enhance its performance.

The Balance Sheet

A typical balance sheet looks like this:

Table I - 1

Balance Sheet for 1992

Current Assets		**Current Liabilities**	
Cash	$194,900	Accounts Payable	$146,200
Receivables	243,600	Notes Payable	194,900
Inventory	730,800	Other Current Liabilities	97,400
Total Current Assets	$1,169,300	Total Current Liabilities	438,500
Property, Plant & Equipment	$1,339,750	Long-Term Liabilities	194,900
		Total Liabilities	633,400
Less Depreciation	803,850	Stockholders' Equity	1,071,800
Net Property & Equip.	$535,900	Total Liabilities &	
Total Assets	$1,705,200	Stockholders Equity	$ 1,705,200

Five Basic Areas of the Balance Sheet

1. Current Assets:
   Current assets are cash or assets that will usually be turned into cash in less than one year. Some examples of current assets are:

- Accounts receivable: amounts due to the firm from sales made to customers

- Inventory: items in a warehouse or stocked in a store awaiting sale in the ordinary course of operation

In the balance sheet shown above current assets are: cash — $194,900; accounts receivable — $243,600; inventory — $730,800; comprising total current assets of $1,169,300.

2. Property, Plant and Equipment:
   Property, plant and equipment, sometimes called fixed assets, are such things as buildings, machinery and vehicles used to generate revenue for the business but not for sale in the normal course of business activity. Net fixed assets simply are fixed assets minus their accumulated depreciation. As fixed assets are used, they usually decline in usefulness and are depreciated. (Depreciation will be discussed more fully in the income statement section.) Net fixed assets in the example above is $535,900. The total assets of $1,705,200 is the combination of total current assets — $1,169,300 — and net fixed assets — $535,900.

3. Current Liabilities:
   Current liabilities are debts owed to others that will ordinarily be paid within one year of the balance sheet date. All forms of debt are claims against the company's assets. The classification as current or long-term depends on the debt's maturity date in relation to the balance sheet date. As shown in the balance sheet example, this includes accounts payable, notes payable and other current liabilities.

   - Accounts payable refers to goods, services and supplies purchased for use in the business operations that have not yet been paid for. Examples of items purchased on account are raw materials used in manufacturing goods for sale and supplies used indirectly for production of goods or services.

- Notes payable are short-term obligations, possibly to a bank or other financial institution, that are payable in one year or less.

- Other current liabilities are other obligations of the firm, such as income tax payable or interest payable, that are not classified as accounts payable or notes payable. The example on page 4 shows: accounts payable — $146,200; notes payable — $194,900; other current liabilities — $97,400; total current liabilities of the firm — $438,500.

4. Long-Term Liabilities:
Long-term liabilities, like short-term debt and accounts payable, are claims against the firm's assets. Long-term debt often takes the form of mortgages or bonds that the firm has issued to help finance its current operation and new acquisitions of property, plant and equipment.

   - Mortgages are a form of debt secured by specific assets.

   - Bonds may take a variety of forms or have a variety of features such as:

     a. Debenture bonds, which are bonds not secured by specific assets of the firm. However, like other unsecured debt, they are secured by assets not specifically pledged to other debtholders.

     b. Convertible bonds, which are bonds that may, under certain conditions, be converted into common stock. At the option of the bondholders, the bonds may be converted or given up in exchange for a specified number of shares of common stock. Typically, convertible bonds are issued by firms whose stock prices are low, but whose management expects growth in the stock prices over time, which makes them attractive for bondholders to convert these bonds into stock. This is a convenient way for firms to grow: first using convertible bonds, then growing so that stock prices increase and bondholders convert. Then the process may start all over again with a new bond issue.

c. Subordinated debentures, which are debenture bonds that are secondary in their claims on the firm's assets and income to other bonds.

d. A sinking fund, which is a provision that requires the firm to retire a portion of its debt each year. This may be done by purchasing bonds in the market or calling bonds from the bondholders at a specific price. Callable bonds may be "called" or purchased from the bondholders at a previously agreed upon price over a specified period of time.

e. The indenture (not to be confused with debenture), which is the agreement between the firm's bondholders and stockholders that includes all of the features or restrictive covenants. Unlike short-term creditors such as those who have sold to the firm on account, bondholders have a much longer-term relationship with the borrower and must have protection against material changes in the firm's financial position.

f. The interest on debt, which is a tax deductible expense that is a very important consideration since this reduces the after-tax cost of debt. Long-term debt is generally defined as debt that has a one-year life or longer.

5. Equity:
   In the example on page 4, the stockholders' equity is $1,071,800. Stockholders' equity represents claims against the assets of a business by its owners. For corporations, stockholders' equity represents the fundamental foundation of ownership in the firm, but the equity section of the balance sheet may also include preferred stock, additional paid-in capital, retained earnings and treasury stock.

   - Preferred stock issued by the firm has preference in terms of claim on income earned and assets over common stock. Preferred stock typically has a stated dividend payment (percentage or dollar amount). Preferred stockholders, however, are not the firm's primary shareholders as the common stockholders are.

     Examples of long-term debt common to small businesses include Small Business Administration (SBA) loans, consumer lines of credit from a financial institution, notes payable to owners, etc.

   - Additional paid-in capital is simply amounts paid in excess of par or stated values of the common or preferred stock.

   - Retained earnings is the accumulated earnings and losses less dividend distributions that the firm has had since its beginning. A common misunderstanding about retained earnings is that, since it often appears on the balance sheet, it is available as cash for the firm to spend. These earnings are distributed throughout the assets of the firm, and many dollars of retained earnings are <u>not</u> held in the form of cash. It is merely a balancing factor in the financial statement.

   - Treasury stock is stock that was issued by the firm, then reacquired, but not formally retired by the firm. Its cost is subtracted from the total of all other stockholders' equity items.

- Dividends on common stock is not a tax deductible expense.

6. Claim on Income and Assets:
Owners and creditors have a claim on assets and the firm's income. These claims vary widely depending on how the claim is secured, securities laws and specific agreements.

- Creditors — Creditors have first claim on income and assets of the firm. The extent of these claims varies. For example, bondholders may be either debenture, mortgage or subordinated bondholders. Those holding debentures have a general claim on the firm's income and assets, but do not have a claim on the firm's specific income or assets. On the other hand, mortgage bonds will be backed by specific assets of the firm pledged as security to the bondholders. If the firm defaults on payments to mortgage bondholders, the specific asset used to secure the mortgage may be liquidated to pay off the debt.

  Small businesses often have a simpler equity structure. Often, the equity section of the balance sheet consists of an owner's capital account and a retained earnings account, in contrast to the complexities of a public company's equity structure as described earlier. The owner's capital account is a substitute for structuring the ownership using capital stock. A capital account can be maintained for each owner to provide separate accounting for his or her respective contributions and withdrawals of equity from the business.

  There may also be subordinated debenture holders who have a claim on income or assets that are subordinate or lower in status than some other bondholders'. Generally, bondholders must receive their interest payments, and the firm must meet the other stipulations of the indebtedness, or the firm will be considered in default. In the case of default, the firm may be required to allow bondholders to have a claim on the assets and even possibly a role in the management of the firm. Except for the default situation, creditors usually have no overt role in the firm's management. They only have an impact on management through the restrictive covenants in the bond indenture clauses or through other credit agreements.

- Preferred stockholders — Preferred stockholders have a claim on income and assets that is secondary to bondholders but ahead of common stockholders (common equity holders). Preferred stockholders are appropriately named since they have a preference in their claims to income and assets over the common stockholders. These stockholders are usually paid a set dividend and any additional dividend payments stipulated in the stock agreement.

  It is important to note, however, that even though preferred stockholders have a claim on income and assets, failing to make a preferred stock dividend payment is not like failing to make a bond interest payment. Generally, preferred stockholders must be paid their dividends before common stockholders are paid theirs, but unlike interest, dividends are not required. Typically, preferred stockholders do not have a role in the management of the firm unless there is a violation in the agreement between the preferred stockholders and the common stockholders. In that case, there may be stipulations in the stock agreement that allow them to have a voice in management.

- Common stockholders — Common stockholders are the firm's primary owners. This is a very important concept that is often overlooked. Just like the sole proprietors of individually owned businesses or the partners in a partnership, the common stockholders are the residual owners, the ones the managers work for. Common stockholders, unlike both bondholders and preferred stockholders, are referred to as residual equity holders because they claim what is left over after bondholders, other creditors and preferred stockholders have made their claims. Because common stockholders have a residual position, they are the primary risk-takers and have the greatest role in the firm's management. Common stockholders elect the board of directors, who select the management of the firm. Although common stockholders often receive dividends, it is not a requirement for them to be paid. As a result of their risky positions, common stockholders expect higher returns on their investment than either bondholders or preferred stockholders.

Significant Facts to Remember About the Balance Sheet

1. The balance sheet must balance. Assets must equal liabilities plus owners' equity as shown in the balance sheet in Table I-1, page 4.

2. Current assets are cash and other assets that are typically used up or turned into cash during an accounting period in the regular course of operation. Property, plant and equipment are not a direct source of cash inflow.

3. Current liabilities will typically be paid off within one year. Long-term debt will remain outstanding longer and will generally not be paid off within a short period of time.

4. Equity in the firm may take many forms: common stock, preferred stock, additional paid capital or retained earnings. Treasury stock is subtracted from total stockholders' equity. However, the primary ownership interest of a corporation is through the common stockholders. Common stockholders are also referred to as residual equity holders because they have the

last claim on income and assets.

5. Retained earnings do not exist in the firm in the form of cash. Retained earnings are distributed throughout the firm's assets and cannot be relied upon when considering cash transactions.

6. Since the balance sheet is a picture of the firm at a particular point in time, taking a snapshot at a different point in time may present a very different picture of the firm.

The Income Statement

The income statement tells how the firm has done over a particular time period. It shows the revenues the firm has earned and what expenses the firm incurred. A very important concept is accrual accounting. Accrual accounting matches the expenses incurred by the firm with the revenue generated in a particular period of time. It is important to understand this concept since accrual accounting is very different from the cash method of accounting. For example, when a firm buys an asset such as a new piece of equipment, that piece of equipment may be used for more than one accounting period. If the equipment is used to generate revenues over a 10-year period, under the accrual accounting method that piece of equipment would depreciate over 10 years. This allocates the expense of using the equipment to the revenues it generated over that 10-year period.

With the cash method of accounting, the cost of the equipment would be charged to expense when it was paid for. In this system, the goal is to make income statements more consistent with what the firm is actually doing from an expense and revenue standpoint. It is very misleading if the firm bought the machine and expensed the entire item in one period but used it over a 10-year period to generate revenues. To avoid this kind of distortion, we will use the accrual accounting method in this handbook.

A simple income statement for a manufacturing firm looks like this:

TABLE I - 2

Income Statement for the Year Ended December 31, 1992

Sales			$2,436,000
Cost of Goods Sold:			
Materials	$925,500		
Labor	584,600		
Heat, Light & Power	87,700		
Indirect Labor	146,200		
Depreciation	53,600		1,797,600
Gross Margin			638,400
Operating Expenses:			
Selling Expenses		$243,600	
Administrative Expenses		280,600	
Total Selling & Administration Expenses			524,200
Income Before Interest and Taxes			114,200
Interest Expense			11,700
Net Income Before Taxes			102,500
*Income Taxes			40,000
Net Income			$ 62,500

This example makes it relatively simple to analyze what is right or wrong about the firm in later chapters without having to make an excessive number of computations.

Let's look at each of the accounts on the income statement.

1. Sales:
   This includes all sales made by the firm during this particular accounting period, 1992. Notice in this statement there is only one sales amount: $2,436,000. In other financial statements it may be important to specify the sales of different products or product lines to provide a more detailed analysis.

2. Cost of Goods Sold:
   Cost of goods sold in this particular income statement includes items that are related to the cost of producing or purchasing the goods that were sold during that accounting period. Production costs consist of materials and labor directly associated with the final product and manufacturing overhead. Manufacturing overhead includes items such as light and power, indirect labor and the depreciation charged production during that accounting period for the equipment used in producing the goods that were sold. The total cost of goods sold, in the example, is $1,797,600.

3. Gross Margin:
   Gross margin consists of sales minus the costs of goods sold. In this case it is $638,400. Gross margin represents the mark-up over the cost to produce or acquire the items sold in that period.

4. Operating Expense:
   Operating expense refers to expenses incurred in producing revenue in a specific time period that lack the direct cause and effect relationship of cost of goods sold and sales. These expenses are associated with a period of time rather than with the product.

   - Selling Expenses:
     The expenses of selling the product in Table I-2 on page 13 amounted to $243,600 during the accounting period. You can divide this into geographical areas, types of products, etc., if necessary for managerial purposes.

   - Administrative Expenses:
     General administrative expenses of the firm cost $280,600 this period. This includes executive salaries (except the sales force), clerical help and all other costs associated with general administration of the firm's activities.

5. Income Before Interest and Taxes:
   Earnings before interest and taxes in the example from page 13 is

$114,200. This is important since the organization must have enough income to meet its interest payments and pay taxes. This is also an important measure of the firm's operations before considering its financing obligations and taxes.

6. Interest Expense:
   Interest expense, a tax deductible item, is $11,700 in the example. This expense includes interest incurred on all types of debt.

7. Net Income Before Taxes:
   Net income before taxes is $102,500 and reflects revenues from sales minus the cost of goods sold, selling expenses, general and administrative expenses and interest expenses. Taxes are then deducted. Federal income tax is shown as 39 percent.

8. Net Income:
   Net income, or what is often referred to as "the bottom line," is $62,500.

The income statement you use for managerial purposes may differ from the ones used for tax purposes or external reporting purposes. Understand that this is not an attempt to be misleading. It is important to know what each set of statements can be used for and that they are designed for that purpose.

Financial Accounting

External reporting requirements may differ significantly from internal ones. Accounting standards exist to meet this very important external reporting requirement. The Financial Accounting Standards Board (FASB) is a seven-member group appointed by the Financial Accounting Foundation to establish these financial or external reporting standards. The FASB issues "Statements of Financial Accounting Standards," commonly referred to as FASBs, which are identified with a number following them such as FASB No. 95. These standards make up the most generally accepted accounting standards.

Managerial Accounting

Financial statements prepared for external purposes may be somewhat helpful to a manager. Most likely you will want more detailed financial statements for internal management purposes. Managerial accounting deals with the financial statements necessary for internal planning and control by the firm's managers. Different managers have a need for different types of information and in different formats. Managerial accounting does not need to adhere to the strict FASB's standards.

Significant Facts to Remember About the Income Statement

1. Income statements contain the revenues and expenses incurred by a firm in a particular accounting period.

2. The income statement should contain as much detail as possible for internal management purposes. This includes itemizing revenues and expenses. This is also helpful in analyzing the statements.

3. Accrual accounting net income differs from the cash basis because of such items as sales that have been made but not yet collected (accounts receivable), purchases made but not yet paid for (accounts payable) and equipment purchased with cash where the expense (depreciation) is distributed over the life of the asset. Net income does not necessarily represent cash.

4. If income statements include some extraordinary item, either revenue or expense, a footnote explaining the item is necessary. An extraordinary item is a particular revenue or expense that is not likely to recur.

5. The income statement is much like a report card. It not only tells how the firm did but may give some indication why. However, a great deal of additional information is needed to understand precisely why the income statement turned out as it did.

6. It is important to remember that the interest on debt is a tax deductible expense and should be included on the income statement. Dividend payments made to stockholders are not operation expenses and are not tax deductible. They should not be included in the income statement, but they do represent an outflow of cash.

THE CASH FLOW STATEMENT

In today's competitive business environment, cash flow analysis has become increasingly important as firms have to rely on their internal cash management for business expansion as opposed to competing with other businesses for the limited amount of capital available from lenders, investors, venture capitalists, etc. Managing cash flow transcends all areas of a business — accounts receivable collection, payments to vendors, timing of purchases and subsequent sales of inventory, etc. Cash flows are also important to monitor when planing for the servicing of long-term debt obligations, especially in highly leveraged companies. For a new business, not having the cash to make interest and principal payments on loans can lead to bankruptcy.

Unlike the typical income statement (based on the accrual method of accounting), a cash flow statement measures the cash that comes in (cash inflows) and that goes out (cash outflows) of a business.

A typical cash flow statement appears on the next page.

Table I-3

Statement of Cash Flows for the Year Ended December 31, 1992

Cash Flows from Operating Activities	
Net Income (from Table I-2)	$ 62,500
Add (or deduct) items not affecting cash:	
Depreciation Expense	53,600
Decrease in Accounts Receivable	10,500
Increase in Accounts Payable	15,400
	79,500
Net Cash Flows from Operating Activities	142,000
Cash Flows from Investing Activities	
Sale of Land	5,000
Purchase of Equipment	(170,000)
Net Cash used by Investing Activities	(165,000)
Cash Flows from Financing Activities	
Payment of Cash Dividends	(50,000)
Issuance of Bonds	100,000
Net Cash Proceeds from Financing Activities	50,000
Net Increase in Cash	27,000
Beginning Cash Balance	167,900
Ending Cash Balance	194,900

A statement of cash flows is useful because it provides answers to the following simple but important questions about the company:

1. Where did the cash come from throughout the period? (year, quarter, month)

2. What was the cash used for during the period?

3. What was the change in cash balance during the period?

Unlike the balance sheet and income statement, the cash flow statement provides a summary of all the cash operating, investing and financing activities. Examples of transactions which fall into each of the categories of activities are:

Operating
Cash Inflows
From sales of goods or services
From returns on investments (interest on loans or dividends on securities)

Cash Outflows
To vendors for inventory
To employees for labor
To banks for interest on loans

Investing
Cash Inflows
From sale of fixed assets (property, plant and equipment)
From collection of principal of loan to other parties

Cash Outflows
To purchase fixed assets
To make loans to other parties

Financing
Cash Inflows
From issuance of bonds
From sale of capital stock

Cash Outflows
To shareholders as dividends
To redeem bondholders

As you can tell from these sample transactions, there is a pattern to determine where a transaction should be categorized on a statement of cash flows. Operating activities is where all transactions that do not fall into the other categories should be placed. It generally includes income statement items as adjusted to arrive at cash-basis income. Investing activities typically relate to changes in long-term assets (like fixed assets), and financing activities involve cash flows from changes in long-term debt and equity items on the balance sheet.

Let's look at each section of the cash flow statement provided in Table I-3.

1. Cash Flows from Operating Activities:
   The cash flows from operating activities converts net income (based on the accrual method of accounting) to net cash flow by eliminating non-cash revenues and non-cash expenses. For example, the depreciation expense of $53,600 (a non-cash expense) must be added back to net income to arrive at net cash flows.

2. Net Cash Flows from Operating Expenses:
   Additionally, changes in accrued accounts adjust net income to cash flows. For example, in Table I-3, accounts receivable decreased $10,500 from the beginning of the year to the end of the year. This $10,500 represents increased cash collections of sales that were "accrued" into income as sales in another period but not collected as cash until the current period.

3. Cash Flows from Investing Activities:
   The investing activities include transactions related to assets held by a company in order to produce its product or to provide its service. For example, a company purchases additional manufacturing equipment to expand production, decreases cash flows in the current period to hopefully increase operating cash flows in the future in the form of added sales volume.

4. Net Increase in Cash:
   After all the "cash-basis" adjustments have been made to net income, the result is the net increase (or decrease) in cash.

5. Beginning and Ending Cash Balance:
   The bottom portion of the cash flow statement reconciles the cash account from the beginning of the year to the end of the year. This acts as "proof" of the accuracy of the cash-basis adjustments. The ending cash balance should equal the cash balance on the balance sheet.

Significant Facts to Remember About the Statement of Cash Flows

1. For many analysts of financial information, cash flows provide a better standard to evaluate operating success, liquidity and financial health. Currently experts feel that the accrual basis of accounting has become too arbitrary to represent valuable data for analysis.

2. The cash flow statement provides a detailed summary of all of the company's activities for the year — operating, investing and financing.

3. Preparing and analyzing a statement of cash flows requires a comparative balance sheet (showing changes in accounts), a

current income statement and other detailed financial information if necessary.

4. Managers should analyze cash flows as often as other financial statements (if not more often) because it is critical that a company continually monitors its ability to meet operating needs.

ANALYZING FINANCIAL STATEMENTS

In this chapter the emphasis is on understanding how to analyze financial statements and use them to find out what is right or wrong about a firm's financial operations and why. Financial statements become more informative when the user analyzes the relationships of particular accounts or groups of accounts in those statements. The information is further enhanced if these analyses are compared over a series of years or to benchmark norms developed from financial statements of a representative sample of several firms in the same industry. This chapter explains the basic techniques of financial statement analysis using ratios and common-size statements.

Ratios are simple comparisons of one item to another to express the size of an item in relation to the other. For example, a ratio of sunny days to rainy days requires that the number of sunny days be divided by the number of rainy days. This chapter divides 16 of the most commonly used ratios into three groups that comprise the main thrust of financial statement analysis.

Common-size statements express every item on the statement as a percentage of some base, usually total assets on the balance sheet and revenue on the income statement.

Liquidity Ratios

Liquidity ratios are designed to show how liquid or cash-free the firm is. In other words, its ability to cover current debts out of cash reserves or other available assets. When someone asks, "How liquid is this firm?" or "How liquid is this asset?" it means how quickly can it be converted into cash.

> Current Ratio — A current ratio of the firm is the ratio of current assets to current liabilities and is computed as follows:

$$\text{Current Ratio} = \frac{\text{Current Assets}}{\text{Current Liabilities}}$$

The current ratio gives some indication of the firm's ability to pay its current liabilities when they come due. Generally, you would expect the current ratio to be larger than one (1). However, what the current ratio should be is based on industry standards, the firm's experience in the business and a number of other factors that will be discussed in the analysis section.

Current assets are resources such as cash, accounts receivable, inventories and other assets that typically will be converted into cash in less than a year. Current liabilities include accounts payable, notes payable and other liabilities that will be paid off within a year. The ability to pay these obligations rests largely on the firm's ability to generate cash from current assets.

> Quick or Acid-Test Ratio — The quick or acid-test ratio consists of dividing current assets, minus inventory, by current liabilities.

$$\text{Acid-Test Ratio} = \frac{\text{Current Assets - Inventory}}{\text{Current Liabilities}}$$

The acid-test ratio takes analysis of the firm's liquidity one step further. By subtracting inventory from the current assets, then dividing by the current liabilities, the least liquid asset is removed. This allows you to determine the firm's ability to pay its liabilities using assets that are cash or only one step away from cash. For example, collection of accounts receivable or sale of marketable securities generates cash in only one step. Inventories have not passed the test of being sold and therefore are not quite as liquid as other current assets. Expect this ratio to be less than the current ratio when inventory is among the assets.

Individual Current Asset Ratio — These ratios are not commonly found in textbooks, but are very convenient to use. Divide each individual current asset by total current liabilities.

$$\text{Individual Current Asset Ratio} = \frac{\text{Each Individual Current Asset}}{\text{Current Liabilities}}$$

This ratio lets you look at each individual current asset and determine its relationship compared to total current liabilities. For example, if the firm has a great deal of cash relative to current liabilities, it can comfortably pay current liabilities when they come due. If the firm has a small amount of cash and a large amount of accounts receivable that may come in after the current liabilities are due, there may be some cause for concern if there is doubt about the collectability of the accounts or if collections are slow.

If the firm has a large inventory relative to current liabilities and not much cash or accounts receivable, it may be very difficult for the firm to meet its current liabilities as they come due. The inventory must first be sold, and the resulting accounts receivable collected. Each of these two steps requires time. This breakdown of the current ratio into individual current asset ratios provides additional help in analyzing the firm's liquidity.

The current ratio, acid-test ratio and individual current asset ratios are static measures; that is, each measures the relationship that exists at a particular point in time, not over a period of time. While this information is important in assessing the adequacy of the amount of existing current assets, it does not reveal anything about when cash will be available as it flows through the accounts. A question of considerable importance is whether or not the normal flow of funds from cash to inventory to accounts receivable and back to cash is sufficiently regular and sizable to enable the firm to pay its debts on time.

Most current liabilities are incurred in the normal course of acquiring goods and services for the firm's operations. Inventory acquired this way is converted to accounts receivable when it is sold. Collection of accounts receivable provides the firm with the cash for payment of liabilities. To assess the timing of this process, the average length of time it takes to collect receivables and sell inventory must be computed. Such information measures the activity within the period's operations, and these calculations are generally referred to as asset utilization, activity ratios or turnover measures. These activity measures are helpful in judging the efficiency with which the firm uses its current assets.

Asset Utilization, Activity Ratios or Turnover Ratios

Asset utilization, activity ratios or turnover ratios help determine how effective the firm is in utilizing its assets in the management of the firm. Often you will see these ratios referred to as activity ratios or turnover ratios. The term "turnover ratios" is used less often because it seems inappropriate for some ratios and does not accurately describe what is taking place.

Inventory Turnover Ratio — The inventory turnover ratio is figured by either dividing sales or cost of goods sold by the average inventory the firm holds. While both sales and cost of goods sold are used in the calculation, they give different results because sales exceed cost of goods sold by the amount of the gross margin. Most sources providing comparison ratios use sales so figures may be compared to published industry norms. The firm's sales take place over the entire year, while inventory level is computed at a specific point in time. Therefore, it is necessary to use the average inventory over the year. Usually this is done by taking the beginning inventory plus the ending inventory and dividing by two.

$$\text{Inventory Turnover Ratio} = \frac{\text{Sales}}{\text{Inventory}}$$

Essentially, this ratio attempts to show, relative to average inventory, what kind of sales are being generated. This gives you an idea of whether you are carrying too large an inventory relative to sales.

In a manufacturing firm, inventory turnover can be greatly affected by technology and efficiency. It is easy for a business to accumulate inventory and reduce its turnover to an unacceptable level. This can result in the accumulation of goods that cannot be sold or that could deteriorate in quality during storage, resulting in losses to the firm. This ratio simply lets you know if you are maintaining enough inventory to support sales or if you have excess inventory.

Accounts Receivable Turnover — Accounts receivable turnover ratio is computed by taking annual credit sales only and dividing them by average accounts receivable.

The ratio will look like this:

$$\text{Accounts Receivable Turnover} = \frac{\text{Annual Credit Sales}}{\text{Average Accounts Receivable}}$$

The accounts receivable turnover ratio gives you some idea of how efficiently you are managing your accounts receivable. If your accounts receivable turnover ratio is too low, it may indicate that you are extending credit terms that are too generous. On the other hand, be aware that you must offer competitive credit terms or you will not have sales. This ratio is essential in managing your accounts receivable and credit sales operation and should be watched carefully.

Credit sales are used because they generate accounts receivable. As in the computations of the last ratio, use averages to avoid distortions that occur when using just one accounts receivable amount at a particular point in time.

Average Collection Period — The average collection period is computed by dividing average accounts receivable by the annual credit sales, which have been divided by 360.

$$\text{Average Collection Period} = \frac{\text{Accounts Receivable}}{\text{Annual Credit Sales} / 360}$$

Dividing annual credit sales by 360 gives us credit sales per day. Then, by dividing accounts receivable by credit sales per day, you get an idea of how long it takes, on average, to collect your accounts receivable. The same information may be obtained by dividing the accounts receivable turnover by 360. The average collection period is one more important measure in determining how well you are managing your accounts receivable. If the average collection period is too long, you must consider the steps necessary to reduce it or make sure you are not giving credit terms that are too liberal.

A basic method of evaluating this ratio is to compare it to the credit terms the firm extends. For example, if the ratio is 45 days and the firm extends credit of 30 days, the firm either has an incorrect credit policy or is not collecting its receivables on a timely basis. Again, like the accounts receivable turnover ratio, you must be extremely careful in analyzing this ratio. If the average collection period is longer than you think it should be and you immediately cut back credit, it may cost you dramatically in the amount of sales you can make. Remember that in managing your accounts receivable there are two sides to the coin: what your competitors are doing and the kind of credit terms you must offer to make the sales you deem necessary.

Profitability Ratios

By using a number of different accounts including sales, total assets and stockholders' equity, profitability ratios give an indication of how effective the firm is in generating profits. Profitability ratios are critical to managers. There are six ratios in this category, each of which gives a different perspective of profitability.

Gross Profit Margin Ratio — The gross profit margin ratio is computed by dividing sales minus cost of goods sold by total sales.

$$\text{Gross Profit Margin Ratio} = \frac{\text{Sales - Cost of Goods Sold}}{\text{Total Sales}}$$

This ratio gives you an idea of how you are managing your sales and the cost of goods sold relative to sales. By looking at sales minus only one expense, cost of goods sold, you take the initial step in determining the firm's profitability. If you cannot manage cost of goods sold, which in a non-service operation is a very high-cost item relative to other expenses, it will greatly reduce your chances of making a high net profit. You should clearly understand that the gross profit margin ratio is the first step in looking at your profitability.

Net Profit Margin — The net profit margin ratio is computed by dividing net profit by sales.

$$\text{Net Profit Margin} = \frac{\text{Net Profit}}{\text{Sales}}$$

Notice that this ratio does not specify whether net profit is before or after taxes. You will find this ratio computed both ways. Depending on your circumstances and preferences, you determine which way you want to compute it. This ratio takes out all expenses, then looks at how "the bottom line" net profit compares to sales. Net profit, in many cases, is considered one of the most important aspects of judging a business' success. The ratio of net profit to sales, or the net profit margin, is extremely critical in evaluating how a firm is doing. It does not, however, show you why the net profit came out as it did relative to sales. We will consider this later in our analysis.

Return on Total Assets — The return on total assets ratio measures the return on total assets (ROA) the firm has made and is computed by dividing net profit by total assets.

$$\text{Return on Total Assets} = \frac{\text{Net Profit}}{\text{Total Assets}}$$

This ratio indicates whether you are effectively utilizing your total assets to generate profit. This is very important in assessing whether you have the correct amount, composition, support sales and assets to generate profitability.

Total Asset Turnover — The total asset turnover ratio is computed by dividing sales by total assets. It indicates the amount of sales you are generating from the firm's total assets. This ratio is a good example of how using the word "turnover" in the name is misleading. In the financial field, this is what the ratio is called. The firm, however, does not "turn over" total assets during a typical accounting period. This ratio is computed as follows:

$$\text{Total Asset Turnover Ratio} = \frac{\text{Sales}}{\text{Total Assets}}$$

This ratio is extremely important in understanding how productive the firm's assets are in generating sales. If the firm has excess assets, it will look as if it is not generating nearly the sales it should from total assets. If, in fact, the firm has the correct amount of total assets but not the sales force or sales it should have, something may be wrong in the sales area. This ratio is very useful as an initial indicator of a problem with sales or an excessive accumulation of assets. The analyst, after seeing this ratio as too low, will know to look further into the lack of a sales effort, a declining market for the goods, increased competition or too large and inefficient an asset base.

Fixed Asset Turnover — The term "fixed assets" refers to the firm's property, plant and equipment shown on the balance sheet. The fixed asset turnover ratio is computed by dividing sales by fixed assets.

$$\text{Fixed Asset Turnover} = \frac{\text{Sales}}{\text{Fixed Assets}}$$

This ratio, like the total asset turnover ratio and inventory turnover ratio, gives additional information about how successfully the firm is generating sales from its various assets. If this ratio is too low, it means the firm has too many fixed assets or is simply not generating enough sales relative to fixed assets.

Fixed assets that are not as productive or efficient as those of more modern companies may cause the firm to have a much lower fixed asset turnover than the more modern, productive companies. Currently, U.S. industry places a great deal of emphasis on the productivity of all the firm's assets, including fixed assets.

Return on Stockholders' Equity — The return on stockholders' equity, or net worth ratio, is computed by dividing net profit by stockholders' equity.

$$\text{Return on Stockholders' Equity} = \frac{\text{Net Profit}}{\text{Stockholders' Equity}}$$

This ratio indicates what kind of profit you have generated on the owners' equity. If you are the owner, this gives you some indication of how productive the business is in generating profits for you. Owners invest in a business and expect to make a return on their investments. This gives them some indication of how well they are doing. The difference between the return on total assets and the return on stockholders' equity occurs because of the debt a firm has in its financial structure.

Leverage Ratios

The term leverage most typically refers to how much debt a firm has. In this case, leverage ratios compare this debt to various other items on the income statement or the balance sheet. It also considers whether interest payments that must be made are covered by current earnings. Leverage ratios are important in determining the likelihood of the firm paying its debt obligations. The more debt a firm has relative to its assets, income producing ability and equity, the more likely it is to have difficulty meeting these obligations. On the other hand, recall that interest payments on debt are a tax deductible expense until dividends are paid to equity holders, thereby providing the firm with a significant tax advantage.

Debt to Total Assets — The debt to total assets ratio is computed by dividing total debt by total assets.

$$\text{Debt to Total Assets} = \frac{\text{Total Debt}}{\text{Total Assets}}$$

As you know from the previous balance sheet, total assets is equal to total liabilities plus owners' equity. Dividing the total debt by total assets reveals the proportion of total assets financed by total debt. Used in conjunction with profitability ratios, this calculation indicates the degree of difficulty the firm might be in if it has a high debt ratio compared to profit. This ratio is commonly used by all groups analyzing a firm's financial statements.

Debt to Stockholders' Equity — The debt to stockholders' equity ratio is determined by dividing total debt by equity.

$$\text{Debt to Stockholders' Equity} = \frac{\text{Total Debt}}{\text{Stockholders' Equity}}$$

This ratio is very important, particularly to the common equity holders or others who have invested in the company. Owners of the firm like to know how much total debt there is relative to how much they have invested. A high ratio indicates that the firm may be "highly leveraged." If a firm is generating substantial earnings on investments (return on assets) that exceed the cost of the debt, then this is a positive position for the common stockholders. On the other hand, if the firm's earnings drop, this can be a very dangerous position for the firm because the cost of liabilities exceeds the amount of profit those liabilities earn.

Times Interest Earned — This ratio is computed by dividing earnings before interest and taxes by interest charges.

$$\text{Times Interest Earned} = \frac{\text{Earnings Before Interest \& Taxes}}{\text{Interest Charges}}$$

The purpose of this ratio is to see if interest charges are covered by earnings before interest and taxes. It is extremely important that this ratio greatly exceed one (1) since the firm may just meet its interest charges or not make them at all if the ratio is one or below. Failure to make interest payments would cause the firm to go into default and result in serious problems with bondholders.

Fixed Charge Coverage — The fixed charge coverage ratio is similar to the times interest earned ratio, but takes into account other fixed charges such as lease expenses that the firm has in addition to interest payments. This ratio is computed by dividing the income available for meeting fixed charges by the fixed charges.

$$\text{Fixed Charge Coverage} = \frac{\text{Income Available for Fixed Charges}}{\text{Fixed Charges}}$$

This information shows how able the firm is to meet fixed charges such as interest payments, leases and possibly even sinking fund payments for debt. (Sinking fund payments are simply payments that must be made to a fund set aside to retire bonds on a fixed schedule or to purchase bonds to retire them.) Funding for sinking funds is made on an after-tax basis. This ratio must exceed one (1) for the firm to stay out of trouble with creditors and leasors.

Ratio Computation

Below are examples of the different ratios we've discussed using information from the income statement and balance sheets on the following pages. In the right-hand column are the industry averages, which will be discussed in the analysis phase. In the left column are our sample firm's ratios. (The ratio computations are shown in Appendix 1 in the back of the text.) It is recommended that you make each computation to better understand how it is done.

Financial Ratios

Ratio	XYZ	Industry Averages
Current	2.67	2.4
Acid Test	1.00	1.10
Average Collection Period	36 days	43 days
Accounts Receivable Turnover	10X[1]	9X
Inventory Turnover	3.33X	9.8X
Fixed Asset Turnover	4.55X	4.6X
Total Asset Turnover	1.43X	2X
Debt/Equity	59.1%	174%
Debt/Total Assets	37.1%	63.5%
Times Interest Earned	9.76	10.6X
Gross Profit Margin	26.2%	27.2%
Net Profit Margin	2.57%	3.3%
Return on Assets (ROA)	3.67%	6.6%
Return on Equity	5.83%	18.1%

[1] indicates times

Before analyzing the financial statements based on the ratios, you need to look at an additional set of computations to make a detailed analysis of the financial statements.

Common-Size Analysis

Common-size analysis attempts to take the dollar-size factor out of comparing financial information.

Income Statement — Performing common-size analysis on the income statement entails dividing all items (except for sales) by sales. This gives you what is often referred to as a "percent of sales" computation. In fact, when you divide each item on the income statement by sales, you have each item expressed as a decimal relative to sales. You must multiply by 100 or move the decimal place two points to the right to change it to a percentage. This is very helpful information since it allows you to scan income statements quickly and look at the percent each item is of sales. Once you get familiar with this technique, it can be very useful and allow rapid evaluation of financial statements.

Balance Sheet — On the balance sheet, all items are divided by total assets. The common-size balance sheet supplements the information obtained from the activity ratios and the return on fixed assets.

Income Statement

			% of Sales	% of Industry Standards
Sales		$2,436,000		
Cost of Goods Sold:				
Materials	925,500		38.0	37.0
Labor	584,600		24.0	24.0
Heat, Light & Power	87,700		3.6	3.5
Indirect Labor	146,200		6.0	6.0
Depreciation	53,600	1,797.600	2.2/73.8	2.3/72.8
Gross Margin		638,400	26.2	27.2
Operating Expenses:				
Selling Expenses		243,600	10.0	10.0
Administrative Expenses		280,600	11.5	10.0
Total Selling & Admin. Expenses		524,200		
Income Before Interest & Taxes		114,200	4.7	7.2
Interest Expense		11,700	0.5	1.0
Net Income Before Taxes		102,500	4.2	6.2
Federal Income Taxes (39%)		40,000		
Net Income		62,500	2.6	3.3

Assessing the Firm's Strengths and Weaknesses

Now you can begin to assess the firm's strengths and weaknesses. Assume that the industry standards given are accurate and appropriate for the income statement.

BALANCE SHEET

	Amount	% of Total Assets
Cash	$ 194,900	11.43
Receivables	243,600	14.28
Inventory	730,800	42.86
Total Current Assets	1,169,300	68.57
Property, Plant & Equipment	1,339,750	78.57
Less: Depreciation	(803,850)	(47.14)
Net Property, Plant & Equipment	535,900	31.43
Total Assets	1,705,200	100.00
Accounts Payable	146,200	8.57
Notes Payable	194,900	11.43
Other Current Liabilities	97,400	5.71
Total Current Liabilities	438,500	25.71
Long-Term Liabilities	194,900	11.43
Total Liabilities	633,400	37.14
Stockholders' Equity	1,071,800	62.86
Total Liabilities & Stockholders' Equity	1,705,200	100.00

The following is an assessment of the strengths and weaknesses of the income statement and balance sheet accounts.

Income Statement

1. Strengths:
   Selling Expenses — Selling expenses are exactly the same as the industry standards, and we will assume them to be either a strength or at least not a weakness at this time.

2. Weaknesses:
   Materials — Materials are running 38 percent of sales as compared to the industry standard of 37 percent. Although this may seem like a minor deviation, one percent on $2,436,000 sales is more than $24,000. When net profit is $62,500, the $24,000 becomes extremely significant because it is almost 40 percent of profits. Therefore, the one percent deviation in materials over the industry standard is a significant weakness.

   Heat, Light & Power — Heat, light and power in this case is running at 3.6 percent of sales, slightly exceeding the industry standard by .1 percent. Again, while this seems very small, if this were down to 3.5 percent, it would contribute nearly another $2,500 to profits.

   Gross Profit — The gross profit of 26.2 percent is lower than the industry standard of 27.2 percent. You can quickly see why gross profit is down a percent over what it should be, given the difficulties with materials, heat, light and power. While depreciation is slightly less than the industry standard, this can deviate based on depreciation methods, the type of machinery and the quantity of equipment and facilities. At this point, we will not consider depreciation either a strength or weakness. Depreciation does, however, change the gross profit figure. You can clearly see that gross profit has suffered by a percentage point primarily as a result of materials, but also as a result of heat, light and power expenses.

General & Administrative Expenses — General and administrative expenses are 1.5 percent higher than they should be relative to industry standards. If you were able to reduce general and administrative expenses to 10 percent and keep other things in line, you would enhance profits by more than $36,000. Again, keep in mind that $36,000, compared to a net profit of over $62,500, is significant to the firm. While 1.5 percent does not seem to be serious at first glance, when it is converted to dollars it becomes significant compared to net profit.

Income Before Interest & Taxes — Income before interest and taxes is only 4.7 percent of sales as opposed to the industry standard of 7.2 percent. You can look at the upper portion of the income statement and see that general and administrative expenses have contributed 1.5 percent; heat, light and power contributed a small amount; and materials contributed one percent. You can look at income before interest and taxes and see that it is clearly 2.5 percent below industry standards. And we know that 2.5 percent of our total sales of $2,436,000 converts to $60,900, which is substantial. A closer look must be taken to see what is going on.

Interest Expense — Interest expense is only half of the industry standard. You must decide whether this is good or bad. Remember what was said earlier: Interest expense is not bad if you are using the lender's money wisely and earning a very positive return on it. On the other hand, if you are not able to borrow when you need money and it is dampening your sales, having too little interest expense may be very bad for the firm. If you borrowed and your sales didn't turn out to be as high as you anticipated or other factors caused your profits before interest payments to be insufficient to cover your debt payments, your firm may face serious consequences. At this point, you must analyze the financial statement further to see whether the interest expense being below the industry standard is good or bad.

Net Profit Before Taxes and Net Profit After Taxes — Net profit before taxes and net profit after taxes is much lower than it should be. Because previous expenses exceeded industry standards, it is clear why the net profit is 2.6 percent compared to the industry standard of 3.3 percent .

Balance Sheet

1. Strengths:

Current Ratio — The current ratio is high, and you need to determine whether this is good or bad. As indicated earlier, this figure gives some indication of the company's ability to pay current debt. Upon initial inspection, the current ratio being somewhat high may appear good. As you recall, however, you must continue with additional tests to see whether this is good or bad. This will be discussed further in combination with other ratios under the weaknesses section.

Average Collection Period — The average collection period is 36 days where the industry standard is 43 days. Upon first inspection, this also appears to be very good. However, having an average collection period much shorter than the industry standard can be good or bad. In this case, you are collecting the accounts receivable faster than the industry, and if this is not hampering sales, then it is a positive. It may indicate you are more efficient in collecting accounts receivable, accurate in setting policies and stimulating early collection. On the other hand, it may indicate that you are being far too restrictive in policies — collecting accounts faster, but possibly losing profitable although slower paying customers as a result.

Accounts Receivable Turnover — The accounts receivable turnover is 10 times as compared to an industry standard of nine times. This, like the average collection period, appears to be good, and it may be; but the same warning that was given for average collection period must be given here.

2. Weaknesses:

   Acid-Test Ratio — The acid test ratio raises some concern. You can see the industry average is 1.10 percent, and the acid-test you have is one percent. Compared with the current ratio of 2.67 percent (industry average 2.4 percent), it looks as if the liquidity position is better than the industry standard. But upon closer inspection, it is clear that the inventory must be larger than others in the industry since taking it out in this computation shows the firm to be lacking in liquidity. This inventory investment will use some cash so that the acid-test ratio may fall below the industry standard. This need for cash may be the reason the accounts receivable turnover is faster and the average collection period is shorter than the industry standard. Without more information you do not know this to be the case, but it is a possibility bearing further investigation.

   Inventory Turnover — The inventory turnover at 3.3 percent is extremely low compared to the 9.8 percent industry average. This may be a major concern to the company. The current ratio was high; the acid-test ratio was low; and the inventory turnover is very low. We can see from these three ratios, large inventories may be a problem. The firm must raise capital to provide assets to operate. If the firm is making excessive investments in inventory, this will cost the firm profits. In this case, the inventory appears to be much too large, which could be a major reason the firm's profits are only about one-third of the industry standard.

   Fixed Asset Turnover — Fixed asset turnover is also slightly lower than the industry average. This is not enough under the industry average to cause major concern. However, it is not something you should ignore. This indicates you are not getting the sales out of the fixed assets that other firms in the industry are.

Total Asset Turnover — Total asset turnover is also below the industry average at 1.43 percent compared to two percent for the industry. You can see that this is a result of inventories turning over too slowly and fixed assets not being quite as productive as those of the rest of the industry. As a result, the sales to total assets is far below the industry average and is cause for a great deal of concern.

3. Strengths or Weaknesses:

Total Debt to Stockholders' Equity — Total debt to stockholders' equity is only 59.1 percent, whereas the industry average is 174 percent. Is this good or bad? Again, you must examine whether having debt is good. Having debt is good if you are using that leverage or debt to your advantage. It is bad if you are incurring unnecessary expenses associated with the debt, which causes you to have a lower profit than desired. Even though your debt is very low compared to the industry standard, you must be using part of it to finance a very large inventory. While not having much debt may be a plus or minus for the firm, the inefficient use of it by financing a large inventory is not good management — unless you can show that a large inventory is necessary, which makes deviations from the industry standard acceptable.

Total Debt to Total Assets — You see that total debt to total assets is only 37.1 percent as opposed to 63.5 percent for the industry. Again, the discussion concerning total debt to total assets is similar to the one concerning total debt to net worth. At this point you are not sure whether it is good or bad.

Times Interest Earned — Times interest earned is 9.7 compared to the industry average of 10. This is somewhat lower than the industry average, but doesn't raise major concerns at this point unless the inventory size suggests that the firm is continuing to manufacture a product it cannot sell. If this is the case, the times interest earned ratio might suddenly get worse.

Looking at the financial ratios from the income statement and the balance sheet, the gross profits to sales are below what they should be, net profit to sales is greatly below what it should be, net profit to total assets is extremely low, and net profit to equity is also extremely low.

Summary of Financial Condition of Firm

Assuming the industry standards are the correct ones against which to measure the firm's performance, here are some of the difficulties this firm has.

1. The inventory is too high and has caused the current ratio to be too high and the inventory turnover to be far below the industry standards. In part, the inventory accounts for sales to total assets to be substantially below industry standards.

2. Materials, as a percentage of sales, are one percent higher than industry standards; heat, light and power are .1 percent too high relative to the industry standards; general and administrative expenses are 1.5 percent too high; gross profit of sales is lower than the industry standard; and net profit to sales is lower than the industry standard.

3. A combination of profit squeeze and a low total asset turnover is a result of the inventory being too large, causing the ratio of net profit to total assets to be substantially below the industry average. The combination of expenses being too high and total assets being too high results in the net profit (as a percentage of total assets) being about two-thirds of the industry standard.

4. Net profit to stockholders' equity is far below the industry standard at 5.83 percent compared to 18.1 percent. Looking at the ratio of debt to stockholders' equity and total debt to total assets, you will see that they are far below the industry standards and that net profit was squeezed from several areas. Examining net profit to stockholders' equity, you see that a combination of

little debt, high equity and low net profits have caused the net profit to the common equity holders to be extremely low.

5. Don't assume that items such as material, heat, light, power and general and administrative expenses are too high. It may be that the very tight credit policy has caused sales to be too low. If sales were higher, all the rest of the ratios could fall into place. It may be that the way you have to buy materials, given the level of sales, caused the cost to be slightly higher. Sales may be causing a great deal of the problem. Low sales would also make the inventory problem appear very great. Look closely at the expense items, the level of debt and assets and the firm's ability to make sales.

Cautions About Ratio Analysis

- Use whatever ratios you think are appropriate. Do not be bound by the ratios given here or found in any other source. If you think a particular relationship is important to the type of analysis you are doing, compute that ratio and develop standards against which to compare it.

- Be careful when using percentages to not misinterpret results. Percentages can often be misleading if you do not understand the actual numbers. For example, if a particular department had an annual turnover rate of 33.3 percent, you might find this very high until you recognized that there were only three people in that department and one of them left.

  Managers can jump to the wrong conclusions by looking at percentages when they do not understand the underlying numbers. A further caution when using percentages: They are not additive if their bases are different. In other words, simply adding 20 percent and 40 percent does not necessarily make 60 percent if you are talking about different basic quantities to start with. In other words, if you have 20 out of 100 or 20 percent in one case and 20 out of 200 or 10 percent in the second case, you cannot assume that 30 out of 300 is 30 percent since the 100 and 200 represent different bases.

- A common mistake is what is called "one period ratio enforcement." It is easy to forget that ratios are computed at a point in time, and you may not want your firm to look continually the same. For example, if you do daily financial summaries that include an income statement and you do a percentage of sales computation for all of the expenses involved, there will be days when some percentages are greatly out of line. This may be a result of the internal policies regarding the issuance of items out of inventory, build-up of inventory or labor related to a particular production run that should be spread over a larger number of units, etc.

  It is very important when using a ratio analysis to understand the numbers and the reasons behind the numbers before you jump to a conclusion. Furthermore, even if the ratios show that the firm is in an undesirable position during a particular accounting period, this may be acceptable during certain periods of the year if there are seasonal factors to consider. Do not force the firm to look the same at all times. For example, your standard labor percentage may be 40 percent of sales, yet during a particular month you know that the ratio of labor expenses to sales will be 60 percent. However, you decide to live with this since you have valuable employees you cannot replace. You would simply stick with your excellent employees and get through the 60 percent month. Other months the ratio may be as low as 30 percent, and your overall annual rate might end up being the 40 percent target. Terminating these employees and then attempting to hire them back would be very poor management and would cause much higher labor costs and a great deal of ill will.

- Be careful when using fixed ratio standards when times are changing. Often the standards that were appropriate for ratios during the first five years of the firm's existence are not appropriate for the second five years, or they might change from year-to-year given labor costs, materials costs, ingredients costs, etc.

- Be sure to use correct standards in your comparison. You can make serious mistakes and disrupt the firm's operations if you use a ratio analysis but have incorrect standards for comparison. Do not assume industry standards are correct. For a new or small business the lack of "industry standards" makes analysis more challenging. These businesses must rely heavily on their own historical information as they gain years of business data. As a starting point, these businesses may have to look to ratio information for a "typical" business in their industries, even if it is much larger.

  Industry standards may not apply to your firm. Use industry standards as a basic guideline, and when you become comfortable and completely understand how your firm operates, establish your own standards. If you live in a market where labor costs are higher than the standards or if cost of materials is higher, this needs to be taken into account in your analysis. Trying to match industry standards can create serious problems and result in gross mismanagement of your firm.

- Another common mistake is thinking that ratio computation is equal to ratio analysis. Computing the ratios is important, but actually analyzing what has taken place within the firm goes far beyond the computation. Often, managers make the mistake of thinking once they have computed the ratios and briefly looked over them, they have analyzed them.

- Using financial ratios to analyze what is right or wrong in a firm only gives you a part of the picture. Although ratios are extremely important in understanding the firm's operations, they must be put in perspective with other information to gain a complete understanding. For example, assume a firm has a cost of goods sold that is two percent higher than its standards. How do you analyze why the costs were too high? Were you pricing the product improperly? Were you buying improperly? It takes a much more in-depth analysis than the financial ratios to fully understand why the results turned out as they did. In other words, it is extremely important for you to understand the firm's operations and not just compute the financial ratios. This is one of the difficulties in having a consultant attempt to analyze what is wrong with your firm without understanding your particular operations.

3

SETTING STANDARDS AND TAKING CORRECTIVE ACTION

If your analysis reveals a problem, it's time to take corrective action. When taking corrective action you need to be aware of what standards have been set, whether the standards are appropriate, whether they can consistently be met during given time periods and what the expectations are when standards are not met. Once you understand what the problems are, through the analysis of the financial statements and other documents, it is important to understand how you arrived at this point. Industry and company standards were established as guidelines to measure performance. Hopefully, a strategy has been established for times when there are variances from these standards. Furthermore, you must consider the impact of the variance and any changes that are made on the organization.

A major consideration when taking corrective action is to understand managerial and behavioral considerations and how change can be implemented so that the results are positive for the organization. Many times, financial managers with new financial analysis tools are all too eager to ignore these important considerations when trying to take corrective action.

In this chapter we will deal with using industry standards, setting company standards, the impact of variations from these standards, the follow-up action when there is a variance from standards and the managerial and behavioral considerations when implementing changes.

Setting Standards

Setting standards that measure performance is absolutely critical to achieving positive results from financial statement analysis. If standards are improperly devised or used, comparison of actual events with standards will be invalid.

Industry Standards—There are a number of helpful and reliable sources that can be used when determining industry standards. Many trade associations and firms publish financial ratios, but following are the three most widely used business and financial resources.

- The first is The Almanac of Business and Industrial Financial Ratios, which gives corporate performance in two tables for each industry. One table reports the operating and financial information for corporations with and without net income. A second table provides the same information for those corporations that operated at a profit. This resource provides a number of ratios displayed in graphic form to aid in understanding the analysis. The source of the data used is U.S. Treasury and Internal Revenue Service information. The almanac defines each ratio, shows how it is computed and provides the source of the information so you know what kind of numbers you are working with. It covers approximately 16 areas of general business categories, with break-outs within each category on a specific industry. The almanac also cross-references each industry with the standard industrial classification of industries (SIC) codes, making it easier for the analyst to determine whether the industry in the SIC is equivalent to the one in the almanac.

- The second source is the Robert Morris Associates Annual Statement Studies. These are often referred to as the RMA Statement Studies. The RMA also cross-references with SIC categories and carefully defines the input into their ratios, the way their ratios are computed and reports ratios in the upper, second, third and fourth quartiles for each industry. The RMA industries are classified into seven broad areas with detail in subcategories within each area. It also provides comparison information for broad industry standards.

- The third source is Dun and Bradstreet. All three of these sources provide very valuable information, but in different formats with slightly different computations for different ways of looking at industries. Those doing financial statement analysis should look carefully at these sources, as well as others, to determine which is the most useful in analyzing their particular firms.

Company Standards — Once you understand the broad industry standards, it is important that you modify this information to make it applicable to your particular firm. Realize that your firm may vary widely from the established industry standards for valid business reasons. Furthermore, understand that industry standards are average ratios of firms and therefore, the average may not precisely fit any one firm. Developing company standards based on experience and carefully watching the ratios over a period of years is necessary before you evaluate a firm's ratios against a set of standards. Company standards may vary widely from industry standards for a number of reasons. These include:

1. Age — The age of a firm may be quite different from the average of the firms reported in the reference material. This age difference may cause cost, revenue streams, life of assets and the cost of assets to differ from industry standards.

2. Location — The location of your firm may have a significant impact on how your numbers compare to industry standards. Your particular industry, real estate and labor may be more or less expensive than industries typically found in the reference material.

3. Managerial Styles — Managerial styles may cause company standards to be very different than industry standards. Different managers may run their operations differently. Some are risk takers and some are risk-averse. Some may save in certain areas and spend in others, which may not be the same as the industry standards, but at the same time, is very effective for that particular firm.

4. Operational Changes — Operational changes can have a major impact on the way financial information looks. For example, if production schedules have been lengthened or shortened or methods of operation changed over a period of time, this may cause the firm's standards to look very different from industry standards.

The setting of a company's standards is as important as the computation and analysis of the ratio. If the standard is wrong, all else is useless and may even be harmful. Financial managers should, therefore, spend a great deal of time establishing what standards are appropriate for their particular companies.

Tips for Setting Your Firm's Standards

- Carefully study your firm's financial history. Establish what ratios stay relatively constant and which ones tend to fluctuate over time.

- Watch for changes in accounting methods that may cause ratios to change but that do not necessarily mean the firm's actual financial position has changed.

- Take into account operating conditions that may make your firm differ from industry standards.
- Review the standards of similar firms if they are available.
- Get employees involved in analyzing information and assisting with standard-setting.
- Be aware of changing conditions that may affect your standards. Adhering to old, inappropriate standards can be very harmful to the firm.

Management Through the Use of Standards

If you want to use standards as an effective management tool, first establish variances from allowable standards and those that cause concern. Acceptable variances still allow you to maintain appropriate performance. The ratios computed in Chapter 2 will help illustrate this process. It was noted that the current ratio was 2.67 compared to an industry standard of 2.4. The difference between the industry standard and the firm's ratio represents an 11 percent deviation from the standard. This is computed as follows:

$$\frac{2.67 - 2.4}{2.4} \times 100 = 11.25\%$$

While in raw numbers the 2.67 did not look far from 2.4, in percentage terms it is. Table III-1 shows each ratio, the industry standard and the percentage deviation from the norm, assuming the industry norm is the firm's standard.

Table III - 1
Ratio Variance

Ratio	Firm's Value	Industry Average	Computation of % Variance	% Variance From Standard
Current	2.67	2.4	$\frac{2.67 - 2.4}{2.4}$ [1]	11.25%
Acid-Test	1.00	1.10	$\frac{1.00 - 1.10}{1.10}$	-9.09% [2]
Avg. Collection Period	36 days	43 days	$\frac{36 - 43}{43}$	-16.28%
Accounts Rec. Turnover	10 times	9 times	$\frac{10 - 9}{9}$	11.11%
Inventory Turnover	3.33 times	9.8 times	$\frac{3.33 - 9.8}{9.8}$	-66.02%
Fixed Asset Turnover	4.55 times	4.6 times	$\frac{4.55 - 4.6}{4.6}$	-1.09%
Total Asset Turnover	1.43 times	2 times	$\frac{1.43 - 2}{2}$	-28.5%
Debt to Equity	59.1%	174%	$\frac{59.1 - 174}{174}$	-66.03%
Debt to Total Assets	37.1%	63.5%	$\frac{37.1 - 63.5}{63.5}$	-41.57%
Times Interest Earned	9.76 times	10.6 times	$\frac{9.76 - 10.6}{10.6}$	-7.92%
Gross Profit Margin	26.2%	27.2%	$\frac{26.2 - 27.2}{27.2}$	-3.68%
Net Profit Margin	2.57%	3.3%	$\frac{2.57 - 3.3}{3.3}$	-22.12%
Return on Assets	3.67%	6.6%	$\frac{3.67 - 6.6}{6.6}$	-44.39%
Return on Equity	5.83%	18.1%	$\frac{5.83 - 18.1}{18.1}$	-67.79%

[1] Each formula is multiplied by 100 to put it in percentage form.
[2] A negative here indicates the firm's ratio is below the industry standard. This may be good or bad depending upon the ratio.

When percentage variations from standards are computed as in Table III-1, some of the percentage variations are large and some are relatively small. When setting up policies or rules governing variances from the standards, it is important to put the variance in percentage form to get the true effect of the magnitude of deviation from standards.

In the example, the variance of fixed asset turnover and gross profit margin may be acceptable, but obviously inventory turnover, total asset turnover, net profit margin, return on asset and return on equity variances are unacceptable. When the variance is as much as 9.09 percent in the case of the acid test ratio, this should cause concern due to its impact on liquidity and its relationship to inventory turnover.

The precise amount of variance tolerated is a matter of judgment based on business conditions, the firm's management, the importance of a ratio at a particular point in time and the ability of the firm to control the variables involved in the ratio.

The Impact of Variances

It is important to understand the impact of a variance from a standard on the organization. A minor variance doesn't warrant a great deal of investigation. On the other hand, if there is a very slight variance that indicates the beginning of a major problem for the company, it should be looked at carefully. Policy measures may need to be established if variances continue to occur over a predetermined period of time. These policies can define what types of corrective action will be taken if a variance exists or becomes habitual.

Managerial Considerations

Using a financial ratio analysis to determine what is wrong with the firm is useless if the firm's management doesn't understand basic management concepts. Management needs to:

- Allow people to participate in goal-setting in the management of the firm.

- Set attainable goals.
- Understand the art of leadership.
- Understand people's resistance to change.
- Coordinate the organization.
- Allow members of the organization to share in the rewards.
- Create cohesiveness in the organization.
- Understand the difference between the long run and short run.
- Understand the implications of various decisions.
- Understand basic behavioral considerations.

Without having a firm grasp on these managerial concepts, managing the firm using ratio standards and trying to get the firm to adhere to these standards is nearly impossible. The following are managerial considerations that must be taken into account when establishing, enforcing and managing the standards established.

Participative Management

Participative management has been both praised and criticized. Participative management is basically allowing individuals to become involved in the managerial decisions of the firm. Done properly, participative management is extremely helpful to establishing goals, reaching these goals and having everyone in the firm working as a team for the best joint effort. For participative management to work, managers must take into account the following concepts:

> Participating Versus Consulting — The manager must allow individuals to participate in a decision versus simply consulting them before a decision is made. This may seem like a fine line, but it is perceived by individuals as a very important difference. Often, managers may consult with individuals without actually allowing them to participate in the decision-making process. It is critical for people to buy into the firm's standards. And they are more likely to do so if they have participated in setting the standards as opposed to simply being consulted about what the standards should be.

Participation Versus Caring — It is often thought that when management cares about what individuals in the firm are doing and has a true concern for their welfare, this constitutes participative management. What is thought to be participative management in this case can actually be paternalistic management. Managers should care about individuals working in the firm, but this does not replace allowing people to actively participate in the managerial decisions of the firm.

Manipulation Versus Participation — Some managers use participative management as a guise to manipulate employees. Participation must take place in an honest, straightforward manner, and managers must not believe that participative management is a tool for manipulating employees. If they do, employees quickly pick this up and usually dismiss any efforts that management makes to let them participate as only a sham.

Setting Attainable Goals

Goal-setting in this context is similar to setting the standards for the ratios we have established. There has been a great deal written about goal-setting. Here, we are dealing with goal-setting relative to the financial standards the firm has set. To ensure that goals or standards are properly set, managers must allow employees to participate in setting these goals; however, there are a number of important considerations to be taken into account.

- Before financial standards are established, they must be clearly thought out, questioned and communicated to everyone so they are understood. Standards that are poorly constructed or not clearly communicated to employees will not be observed and will create more chaos than profitability when management attempts to enforce them. Managers should articulate the standards and make sure they are communicated in a positive and clear way to all employees involved.

- Standards must be attainable yet challenge employees. If standards are not attainable, they will be ignored and meaningless. Employees familiar with the firm will recognize challenging standards that are attainable. Standards should cause employees to stretch their abilities, but at the same time be reasonably attainable. This will help employees improve themselves and feel good about their jobs when they attain their goals.

- Employees must know the implications if standards aren't met. Repercussions must be clearly set forth when the standards are articulated to the employees. This should be done in a non-threatening, positive way. This explanation does not have to be detailed, but should indicate the problems failing to meet standards creates for the firm, the losses the firm may incur and the importance of obtaining the standards.

Leadership

There are as many definitions of leadership as there are people. We all have our own concept of leadership, yet it boils down to getting things done by working with and through employees to achieve organizational goals and standards. There are many facets to leadership. Following are a few tips for providing leadership, helping people accept standards and meeting the firm's financial standards.

Leadership by Example — Leaders must set a good example for other employees to follow. Management should establish its own realistic standards and strive to meet them. When employees see that top managers also have standards they must work to meet and that they have an opportunity to succeed or fail at meeting them, employees will be motivated to meet their own standards.

Openness — Managers must be open, above board and communicate clearly with employees. Managers who play things "too close to the vest" and do not communicate openly with others in the firm are often viewed as suspicious and untrustworthy. Managers must be willing to explain their actions and candidly discuss achievements and failures with employees.

Fairness — Fairness is imperative for good leadership. Managers must be viewed as evenhanded with all employees, but also willing to make exceptions for employees that need special assistance. Fairness does not mean treating all people the same. Fairness involves taking each individual's needs and abilities into account when making decisions about treatment.

Resistance to Change — We know that most individuals are resistant to change, particularly change they did not participate in or do not have control over. When setting standards for the firm and identifying the changes which will be made as a result of failure to meet these standards, it is extremely important to understand how to overcome resistance to change. Managers must create an environment where change is expected, encouraged and rewarded. If management does this, the resistance to change will begin to break down.

Innovation Must Be Rewarded — Innovation must be rewarded and failed innovative efforts not punished. In an environment where innovation is rewarded, people think of new ways to do things and do not fear failure. Thus, the firm will be much less resistant to change.

Avoid the Unexpected — Managers should attempt to avoid unexpected and drastic changes that are unexplained. If a change is anticipated, employees should be informed of the possibility of a change so they are not taken by surprise. This allows employees to avoid the unexpected and to begin adjusting to the change. Often the unexpected is unknown, unfamiliar and frightening. Therefore, every effort must be taken to avoid abrupt, unexpected changes.

Coordination, not Necessarily Centralization — Coordination does not necessarily mean centralization of functions. These are often confused. It is important that all functions that need to be coordinated are coordinated. Coordination involves making sure that the right hand knows what the left hand is doing. Centralization means that someone central to the organization is telling both the right hand and the left hand what to do. These are very different concepts.

Common or Shared Goals Within the Organization — If the organization's financial goals are shared by all, it is easier to achieve them.

Everyone Must Pull His or Her Own Weight — It is important to the manager enforcing standards that everyone pull his or her own weight. If everyone is not doing his or her job and contributing to the organization's overall goals, it will be very difficult to achieve those goals.

Sharing Rewards

If management wants workers to share in the burden of getting the job done and making profits for the company, it must be willing to allow employees to share in the rewards. Participative management means not only allowing employees to participate in the decision-making of the firm, but to participate in the rewards as well. A major failure of many managers is expecting great performance and dedication of employees without properly rewarding them for their efforts. This applies to all levels of the organization.

Share All Rewards — Often employees do not have the opportunity to share in the achievements of the firm. Managers should communicate the firm's success to employees and acknowledge the employees' participation in this success. This does not simply mean reward programs that are standard in many companies, but rewarding employees for all the positive things that happen in a firm. They should share in publicity, financial rewards and upgraded work facilities.

Do Not Be Cheap — If employees perform well, the most

important thing managers can do is to share rewards bountifully. This includes praise for a good job as well as pay increases commensurate with employees' success. If you expect employees to reach the standards you have set, there must be a reward for them to stay interested. Make these rewards valuable enough that when goals are attained, employees achieve satisfaction in doing so.

Cohesiveness

Often in business organizations we overlook the importance of cohesiveness. Cohesiveness involves everyone working together for common goals with a great deal of camaraderie. Here are some tips:

- Cohesiveness is encouraged by employees working in groups. Given proper objectives and coaching, group work greatly enhances cohesiveness.
- Allow workers to share their thoughts on communication, share rewards, set goals and be leaders in the firm. A true feeling of being heard and participating in management will greatly aid in cohesiveness.

Short-Term Versus Long-Term

It is often said that American managers are too short-term oriented, and if they were more long-term oriented, firms would be more successful and would not be at a competitive disadvantage. It is important to understand that managers who are often compensated in the short run look to the short run for rewards. Keep these points in mind when considering this issue.

- Both short-term and long-term goals should be established for employees. This leads to a continuity in performance and an achievement of various goals over a longer period of time. This also allows employees to not only be short-term oriented, which is to their advantage, but also long-term oriented, knowing that if they take shortcuts to enhance their short-term profitability, it will hurt them in the longer term.

- Hold employees accountable for short-term decisions made in previous jobs that produced long-term difficulties. This helps alleviate the problem of employees moving from one job to the next and assuming they do not have to worry about their past performance.

Behavioral Considerations

The way people behave and how their behavior is influenced by other's behavior is crucial for the manager to understand when using financial standards as a management tool. Understanding basic behavioral considerations when dealing with standards can greatly enhance effectiveness. Keep in mind these key points:

1. Stress is created in a variety of ways and is a real factor that managers must deal with. If standards are arbitrarily set or set too high and the repercussion for not meeting the standards is too severe, a great deal of stress may result. It is important for the manager to understand that stress will have a great deal to do with the employee's ability to meet the standards, and therefore, they must be reduced by using some of the managerial considerations already mentioned in this chapter.

   Changes at work cause a great deal of stress with employees. In a study by L. O. Ruck and T. H. Holmes entitled "Scaling of Life Changes: A Comparison of Direct and Indirect Methods," they indicate that being fired from work, business readjustments, change to a different line of work, change in responsibilities at work, trouble with the boss and change in work-hour conditions rank in the top 50 life events causing stress. Stress can be reduced by allowing participative management, setting attainable goals, having good leadership, understanding and managing the resistance to change, keeping the firm coordinated so that the right hand knows what the left hand does, sharing rewards and having a high degree of cohesiveness in the firm.

2. There is and has always been a great deal of controversy about the

role of punishment in managing a firm. Clearly, people's behavior can be modified through punishment, however, it may not be the most effective way to stimulate people. The definition of punishment may be as elusive as that of leadership. An employee may consider himself punished if he or she is simply told not to do something he or she has previously done. On the other hand, if this is handled by a manager with excellent interpersonal skills, the employee may not see this as punishment at all, but as counseling and guidance.

Managers should avoid:

- Criticizing employees in front of others
- Putting employees in a situation where they lose face or are disgraced by their behavior
- Not giving employees the opportunity to explain why they have failed or not met your expectations

Managers should:

- Constructively criticize employees in private
- Give employees an opportunity to explain their points of view
- Offer employees positive advice on how to avoid failure again

3. Employees, especially very efficient ones, can become completely overloaded with work to the point that they become inefficient, upset and manifest problems with their behavior toward other employees or management. Avoid job overload by:

- Properly structuring work so that it may be accomplished
- Staying in constant communication with employees so you know when they are being overloaded
- Allowing employees to plan their work as much as possible to avoid unexpected speed-ups or delays
- Being honest with employees when there is work overload and trying to find a solution

4. Lack of a clear understanding of the work that is expected can create major problems for managers. When setting standards, do not be ambiguous, but make sure the standards are clear and the scope of work understandable.

5. Give constant feedback on the reliability of the standards and the employee's efforts in achieving those standards. Allow employees to give feedback on whether the standards are attainable and realistic.

Behavioral problems with individuals within the workforce can manifest themselves in a variety of ways. Often, behavioral difficulties with employees will show up in their level of work, their ability to attain standards and their interaction with other employees.

When taking corrective action, it is important to review these managerial considerations to produce positive improvements for the firm. Keeping these points in mind will help the financial manager avoid the common mistake of using a new tool such as financial ratio analysis and applying it without understanding basic management concepts. Understanding these basic management concepts and applying them in conjunction with corrective action to meet the established standards of the firm's financial ratios should result in the firm moving forward and becoming more profitable.

4

FORECASTING FINANCIAL STATEMENTS

The importance of forecasting is legendary. Think about what has happened to the oil industry since 1973 and the auto and steel industries in the last decade. If we look at each industry, we see that particular firms have done a better job than others. While it may not have been possible to predict what would take place within each of these industries, with more precise and intensive planning and forecasting it might have been possible to alleviate or avoid the downward turn many industries experienced.

This chapter shows you how to forecast using historical financial information as well as predicted changes in the business. This chapter does not deal with overall strategic planning. That's another book. The purpose of this chapter is to introduce and assist you in the forecasting process as an integral part of strategic planning. Until you thoroughly understand the important role financial statements play in forecasting and developing strategic plans, you will not be able to completely appreciate a firm's strategic planning process. To be effective at financial forecasting, you must keep in mind the following factors:

- Financial statements are report cards that tell what happened. Without additional information you are not always able to tell why it happened. You should use financial statements the way you would use report cards in trying to find out what kind of performance you had, why you had it and what type of performance you will have in the future. Like a report card, you only see the final results. We must use other information to find out what caused the results you received.

- Financial forecasting is an integral part of strategic planning. However, for many managers financial forecasting and analysis isn't clearly understood. Your goal should be to begin to understand the relationship between financial forecasting and strategic planning.

- Financial forecasts, much like strategic plans, are not to be put on the shelf once they are completed. With current computer technology, it is simple to construct forecasts and amend them any time you wish using so-called "what if" statements to see what changes would result if certain data is altered.

- Understand that no one has a crystal ball, so do not be deterred in your efforts to forecast and plan for the future. Often, inexperienced financial managers get frustrated and overly concerned that forecasting is impossible, so they don't even try. If we all knew the future, it would not be very interesting. Our job in this chapter is to use the information from financial statements and other sources to project a reasonably accurate picture of the future.

- A major benefit of financial statement analysis and forecasting is that, while you are struggling to make forecasts, you are forced to think a great deal about the firm's future and the need for additional strategic planning. It is through the process itself that you gain a great deal of insight about the firm's current and future position.

Trend Analysis

In Chapter 2 you read about using trend analysis to see why you are in your current position. In this chapter you will use these trends to forecast the future.

You can begin developing trends in growth rates by looking at income statements and balance sheets. Use income statements over a period of five years to develop trends in growth rates, and use these growth rates to extrapolate future projections. Then return to the balance sheet to see what impact the major changes had. This method:

1. Is simple to compute

2. Is based on the firm's history

3. Extrapolates history into the future as a first try at forecasts

4. Can be made more sophisticated by taking the trend of each revenue or expense into account

5. Can be improved by injecting into the forecasts anticipated changes that will affect the future

To understand the development of growth rate trends, let's take a look at Table IV-1 on the following page.

Table IV-1

Trend Analysis*

	1988	1989	1990	1991	1992
Sales	1,679,000	1,847,000	2,031,700	2,219,500	2,436,000
Cost of Goods Sold:					
Materials	655,700	721,300	778,900	849,000	925,500
Labor	425,900	464,200	496,700	534,400	584,600
Heat, Light & Power	60,500	65,900	71,800	79,000	87,700
Indirect Labor	108,500	115,000	125,400	137,900	146,200
Depreciation	36,600	40,300	44,300	48,700	53,600
Gross Margin	391,800	440,300	514,600	570,500	638,400
Operating Expenses:					
Selling Expenses	161,900	179,800	197,700	217,500	243,600
Administrative Expenses	204,500	220,900	240,700	260,000	280,600
Total Selling & Administrative Expenses	366,400	400,700	438,400	477,500	524,200
Earnings Before Interest and Taxes	25,400	39,600	76,200	93,000	114,200
Interest Expense	8,000	8,800	9,700	10,600	11,700
Net Profit Before Taxes	17,400	30,800	66,500	82,400	102,500
Federal Income Tax (39%)*	6,800	12,000	25,900	32,100	40,000
Net Profit	10,600	18,800	40,600	50,300	62,500

* Rounded to the nearest hundred.

Table IV-1 shows complete income statements from 1988 to 1992. You will use these income statements to develop trends over the last five years with regard to revenues generated from sales and all expenses to operate the business. Why use five years? Why not use six years, 10 years, etc.? There is no magical number. Four or six may be more appropriate, or it may be necessary to use 10. There may be a variety of reasons why statements for more or less than five years are not appropriate. These reasons are easier to understand once you know how to compute the growth rate in these financial statements.

Computing Growth Rates

To learn about trend analysis, take the information contained in Table IV-1 and use it to understand the computations in the Table IV-2. You will attempt to take the growth rate in each individual account from year to year. As an example, using sales from 1988 to 1989, the computation is made as follows:

$$\text{Percentage change in sales from 1988 to 1989} = \frac{\text{1989 sales - 1988 sales}}{\text{1988 sales}} \times 100$$

A simpler way to compute this is:

$$\text{Percentage change in sales} = \frac{\text{1989 sales}}{\text{1988 sales}} - 1 \times 100$$

Look in Table IV-2 on the following page and you will see that the change is 10 percent.

Table IV-2
Growth Rates (in %)[1]

	88-89	89-90	90-91	91-92	Avg.	Proj.
Sales	10	10	9.24	9.75	9.75	10.00
Cost of Goods Sold:						
Materials	10	8	9	9	9	9.00
Labor	9	7	8	9	8.25	8.50
Heat, Light & Power	9	9	10	11	9.75	10.00
Indirect Labor	6	7	10	6	7.75	8.00
Depreciation	10	10	10	10	10	10.00
Selling Expenses	11	10	10	12	10.75	11.00
Administrative Expenses	8	9	8	8	8.25	8.00
Interest Expenses	10	10	10	10	10	10.00

[1] Rounded to the nearest whole percent.

This formula was used to compute the percentage changes in sales for 1988-89, 1989-90, 1990-91 and 1991-92. The average percentage change in sales is 9.75 percent, as shown in the average column in Table IV-2. To get this average you should add the results you have for the change from 1988-89, plus 1989-90, plus 1990-91, plus 1991-92 and divide by 4.

$$\text{1988 - 92 Average \% Sales Increase} = \frac{10 + 10 + 9.24 + 9.75}{4} = 9.75$$

The results are computed for you in Table IV-2. (To compute your answers, use the blank Table IV-2 found in Appendix 2.)

Using Averages Can Be Dangerous

You've observed the percentage growth rates for sales and each particular expense over the five-year period. You've also computed the average of these growth rates (percentage income) over time. Using averages can be very dangerous. When determining the simple average of something, certain anomalies are often overlooked such as large, unusual figures or trends that may be developing that you have not taken into account. We'll look at these problems when we discuss some of the difficulties with using historical assumptions.

Making Projections

Now, let's concentrate on making projections based on the percentage growth rate. In making simple, initial projections based on the historical percentage growth rates, use something you should never overlook in any type of planning or forecasting — common sense. For example, refer to Table IV-2 to look at percentage growth rate in sales over time. From 1988-89 it is 10 percent, from 1989-90 it is 10 percent, then in 1990-91 it dropped to 9.24 percent, and in 1991-92 it is 9.75 percent. The average turns out to be 9.75 percent. The projection is shown as 10 percent. Why not use the average rather than a higher percentage? In every interval the change was nearly 10 percent except during 1990-91 when it was 9.24 percent and clearly pulled the average down. You can adjust the average slightly upward and use the 10 percent projection. Again, it is important to remember that this is only an initial projection based on what you can see from historical information, not taking into account a myriad of other factors. Now look at each individual expense.

Materials — Materials percentage increases have been:

	88-89	89-90	90-91	91-92	Avg.	Proj.
Materials	10	8	9	9	9	9

The initial projection makes sense at nine percent since it was only 10 percent one year then eight percent before leveling off at nine percent in the last two years.

Labor

	88-89	89-90	90-91	91-92	Avg.	Proj.
Labor	9	7	8	9	8.25	8.5

Labor is nine percent in the first and last years of our analysis and seven percent and eight percent during the interim years. The average is 8.25 percent. Using 8.5 percent is a more conservative estimate than using the average for the initial projection since, on the costs side, conservative estimates are always a little higher, and on the revenue side, percentage growths are always a little lower. Use 8.5 percent as your initial projection for labor expense increases.

Heat, Light & Power

	88-89	89-90	90-91	91-92	Avg.	Proj.
Heat, Light & Power	9	9	10	11	9.75	10

Heat, light and power is nine percent growth in 1988-89 and 1989-90, 10 percent in 1990- 91, and 11 percent in 1991-92. You can see that although the average is 9.75 percent, there has been a trend upward so you should use at least 10 percent for your growth rate.

Indirect Labor

	88-89	89-90	90-91	91-92	Avg.	Proj.
Indirect Labor	6	9	10	6	7.75	8

Indirect labor has varied a great deal from six percent in the periods 1988-89 and 1991-92 to as high as 10 percent in the 1990-91 period. Even though the average is 7.75 percent we use eight percent as a conservative estimate.

Depreciation

	88-89	89-90	90-91	91-92	Avg.	Proj.
Depreciation	10	10	10	10	10	10

Depreciation remained at 10 percent in all periods so your initial projection will be 10 percent. Note that depreciation, while an expense, is directly related to the amount of equipment you purchase and the type of depreciation methods you use. In addition, it is a non-cash expense. Depreciation, at this point, is not a great concern.

Selling Expense

	88-89	89-90	90-91	91-92	Avg.	Proj.
Selling Expenses	11	10	10	12	10.75	11

Selling expenses are 11 percent in 1988-89 and 10 percent in both 1989-90 and 1990-91. They then jumped to 12 percent in the 1991-92 interval. The average is 10.75 percent. Using some common sense and because it jumped to 12 percent in 1991-92, make 11 percent for the initial projection.

Administrative Expenses

	88-89	89-90	90-91	91-92	Avg.	Proj.
Admin. Expenses	8	9	8	8	8.25	8.0

Administrative expenses show an eight percent growth rate in every interval except in 1989-90 which is nine percent. The average is 8.25 percent. For your initial projection, use eight percent for increases in general and administrative expenses.

Interest Expenses

	88-89	89-90	90-91	91-92	Avg.	Proj.
Interest Expenses	10	10	10	10	10	10

Interest expenses stayed at 10 percent across the board, so assume that 10 percent is good for your initial projection.

Now we will turn to another commonly used approach to forecasting financial statements.

Percent of Sales Forecast

Percent of sales method simply uses each expense on the income statement as a percent of total sales and makes forecasts based on that. This process is similar to the common size analysis. Use what you already know and simply expand it over a time period.

This method:

1. Is simple to compute
2. Helps you understand the relationship of each expense to sales
3. Serves as a check on other methods of forecasting

Table IV-3 provides the percent each expense is of sales.

Table IV-3

Percent of Sales Forecasts

	1988	1989	1990	1991	1992	Avg.	Proj.
Sales	100	100	100	100	100	100	
Cost of Goods Sold:							
Materials	39.1	39.1	38.3	38.3	38.0	38.6	38.6
Labor	25.4	25.1	24.4	24.1	24.0	24.6	24.0
Heat, Light & Power	3.6	3.6	3.5	3.6	3.6	3.6	3.6
Indirect Labor	6.5	6.2	6.2	6.2	6.0	6.2	6.2
Depreciation	2.2	2.2	2.2	2.2	2.2	2.2	2.2
Selling Expenses	9.6	9.7	9.7	9.8	10.0	9.8	10.0
Administrative Expenses	12.2	11.8	11.9	11.7	11.5	11.8	11.8
Interest Expenses	0.5	0.5	0.5	0.5	0.5	0.5	0.5

To compute your answers, please turn to Appendix 3. Hint: To compute these percentages, use this example:

Materials as a percent of sales for 1988 :

$$\frac{\$655{,}700}{\$1{,}679{,}000} = 39.1\%$$

Round to the nearest decimal point. Make a rule that if the second number to the right of the decimal point is larger than five, round the first number to the right of the decimal point up one. If it is less than five, round down. The averages are computed for you in the far right-hand column of Table IV-3.

The preliminary percentage of sales for 1993 is shown in the last column of Table IV-3.

Materials

	1988	1989	1990	1991	1992	Avg.
Materials	39.1	39.1	38.3	38.3	38.0	38.6

Materials have fluctuated somewhat over time, but have been dropping from 1989 to 1992, with an average of 38.6 percent. Therefore a conservative initial estimate for 1993 would be 38.6 percent.

Labor

	1988	1989	1990	1991	1992	Avg.
Labor	25.4	25.1	24.4	24.1	24.0	24.6

Labor dropped from 25.4 percent in 1988 to 24 percent in 1992. The average is 24.6 percent, but the trend indicates a decline in labor over this period, so use 24 percent as an initial projection.

Heat, Light & Power

	1988	1989	1990	1991	1992	Avg.
Heat, Light & Power	3.6	3.6	3.5	3.6	3.6	3.6

Heat, light and power have remained relatively constant at 3.6 percent in every year except 1990. Use 3.6 percent as the initial projection for 1993.

Indirect Labor

	1988	1989	1990	1991	1992	Avg.
Indirect Labor	6.5	6.2	6.2	6.2	6.0	6.2

Indirect labor declined from 6.5 percent consistently down to 6.2 percent for three years, then to 6 percent in 1992. The average is 6.2 percent, which is a good conservative estimate.

Depreciation

	1988	1989	1990	1991	1992	Avg.
Depreciation	2.2	2.2	2.2	2.2	2.2	2.2

Depreciation has consistently been 2.2 percent of total sales. Use this for your 1993 projection.

Selling Expenses

	1988	1989	1990	1991	1992	Avg.
Selling Exp.	9.6	9.7	9.7	9.8	10.0	9.8

Selling expenses increased from 9.6 percent in 1988 to 10 percent in 1992, with a 9.8 percent average. A conservative estimate for the 1993 projected average would be 10 percent.

Administrative Expenses

	1988	1989	1990	1991	1992	Avg.
Admin. Exp.	12.2	11.8	11.9	11.7	11.5	11.8

Administrative expenses declined from 12.2 percent to 11.5 percent over the 1988 to 1992 period. The average, however, is 11.8 percent. Since there has been quite a bit of variability in this expense, a conservative approach would be to use 11.9 percent as your initial projection for 1993.

Interest Expenses

	1988	1989	1990	1991	1992	Avg.
Interest Exp.	0.5	0.5	0.5	0.5	0.5	0.5

Interest expense has remained a constant 0.5 percent over the five year period. Use 0.5 percent for your initial projection for 1993.

Now that you have the percentage growth rate analysis and the percent of sales, you can begin to make your first forecast. Take a look at Table IV-4 below. You will see the 1992 income statement in the second column. In the third column is the 1993 preliminary forecast.

TABLE IV - 4
Preliminary Forecasts

			Assumptions		
Account	1992	1993 Preliminary Forecasts	% Growth Rate	% of Sales Standard	% of Sales Actual
Sales	2,436,000	2,679,600	10%	100	100
Cost of Goods Sold:					
Materials	925,500	1,008,800	9.0	38.6	37.6
Labor	584,600	634,300	8.5	24.0	23.7
Heat, Light & Power	87,700	96,500	10.0	3.6	3.6
Indirect Labor	146,200	157,900	8.0	6.2	5.9
Depreciation	53,600	59,000	10.0	2.2	2.2
Gross Margin	638,400	723,100			
Operating Expenses:					
Selling Expenses	243,600	270,400	11.0	10.0	10.1
Admin. Expenses	280,600	303,000	8.0	11.8	11.3
Total Selling & Admin. Expenses	524,200				
Earnings Before Interest & Taxes	114,200	149,700			
Interest Expenses	11,700	12,900	10.0	.5	.5
Net Income Before Taxes	102,500	136,800			
Federal Income Taxes (39%)	40,000	53,400			
Net Income	62,500	83,400			

Let's forecast sales for 1993. Table IV-4 indicates that sales in 1992 were $2,436,000. To compute sales for 1993, use the percentage growth rate method of forecasting to make the computation as follows:

1993 Preliminary Sales Forecast = 1992 sales x [1 + computed growth rate]

Using this same type of methodology, the preliminary forecasts for all 1993 expenses are shown in Table IV-4 on the previous page. In column five of Table IV-4, the historical percentage of sales is given. These are based on earlier computations projecting the percentage of sales figures for 1993. In column six of Table IV-4, the percentage of actual sales is given. (To compute your own answers, please turn to Appendix 4.)

Remember that the preliminary 1993 forecast is based on the computed growth rate. This technique was used to forecast the 1993 sales and expenses. It is possible to figure the 1993 sales forecast based on a growth rate, but use the percentage of sales method for all of the expense forecasts. In other words, you could combine approaches and use the growth rate to get sales, then use the percentage of sales method to get all of the expenses forecasted. Instead, percentage growth rates are used for all of the revenues and expenses.

Combining Percentage of Sales and Percentage Growth Rate to Project the Future

Which approach is most appropriate to use for forecasting the future: the percent of sales method, the percentage growth rate or trend analysis? The fact is, a combined approach may be best. In combining these approaches, first compute your preliminary forecasts: in this case for 1993, based on the percentage growth rate. Once you have these numbers, compute each expense as a percentage of sales. You can see how large the percent of sales figures are relative to what they should be. If you get figures for expenses using the trend analysis method that are dramatically out of line with the percent of sales method, you can adjust your figures or rethink what you are doing.

Let's look at this combined approach in Table IV-4 on page 75. You know that with a 10 percent growth rate, you have $2,679,600 in 1993 sales.

Materials — Using a nine percent growth rate on materials, you have $1,008,800. When you compute the percentage of sales method, you get 37.6 percent. This differs from the 38.6 percent you had originally computed as a standard. At this point, you need to decide whether the nine percent growth rate will significantly alter your projections for materials as a percentage of sales. Initially, let's decide that this is within your parameters of acceptability.

Labor — Using an 8.5 percent growth rate, your labor expense for 1993 is 23.7 percent of sales compared to your norm of 24 percent. This demonstrates that it is possible to make reasonable projections using the percentage increase (growth rate) method.

Heat, Light & Power — Using a 10 percent growth rate in heat, light and power, the 1993 projected percentage of sales is 3.6 percent — exactly what was projected using your estimates of the percentage of sales.

It is possible to use the percentage growth rate method for each individual expense and check how it looks relative to your projection. Keep in mind that these are preliminary forecasts and are based exclusively on historical information. This is extremely significant. Forecasting involves much more than simple historical extrapolation. This only tells you what would happen if the future were exactly like the past. Several points must be made about preliminary forecasting.

1. Simple Extrapolation — This means taking historical figures and extending them to the future without major adjustments. In this case, the percentage growth rate method was used to get your 1993 forecast.

2. Weighted Extrapolation — It may be appropriate to use what is commonly referred to as weighted extrapolation. This means you

weigh each year according to its perceived importance to you in making a projection for the future. For example, look at the indirect labor figures on Table IV-2 on page 68. If you use weighted extrapolation, you might use the oldest interval, 1988-89 as the least important with 1989-90 being slightly more important, 1990-91 being even more important and the 1991-92 interval the most important. When considering these from least important to most important, we assigned a weight of one for the 1988-89 interval, a weight of two for the 1989-90 interval, a weight of three for the 1990-91 interval and a weight of four for the 1991-92 interval. The computation for your projection would be:

Weighted extrapolation percentage increase =

$$[w_{88\text{-}89} \times i_{88\text{-}89}] + [w_{89\text{-}90} \times i_{89\text{-}90}] + [w_{90\text{-}91} \times i_{90\text{-}91}] + [w_{91\text{-}92} \times i_{91\text{-}92}]/10$$

$w_{88\text{-}89}$ = weight for 88-89 interval

$w_{89\text{-}90}$ = weight for 89-90 interval

$w_{90\text{-}91}$ = weight for 90-91 interval

$w_{91\text{-}92}$ = weight for 91-92 interval

$i_{88\text{-}89}$ = percent increase for 88-89 interval

$i_{89\text{-}90}$ = percent increase for 89-90 interval

$i_{90\text{-}91}$ = percent increase for 90-91 interval

$i_{91\text{-}92}$ = percent increase for 91-92 interval

Filling in the numbers, it looks like:

Weighted extrapolation percentage increase =

$$\frac{[(1\text{x}6)+(2\text{x}9)+(3\text{x}10)+(4\text{x}6)]}{10}$$

Why divide by 10 when you get an average and use only four

numbers? You have used weights of one, two, three and four, and these total 10. Using this approach, your weighted average extrapolation figure for indirect labor is 7.8 percent. This is not significantly different than taking the simple average which was 7.75 percent. Sometimes this method will cause a large deviation and at other times it will not. It causes a large deviation when current figures are very different from older figures.

3. Caution — You may look at this method and find it intriguing and very logical, but it can also be misleading. We arbitrarily used weighted extrapolation, making the current years most important and the older years least important. This could be the case, but it may not be. You must understand the underlying information. This method is widely talked about but should be used with a great deal of caution unless you fully understand its implications:

   - This method is only applicable if you have devised a way to use the weights for each period correctly.
   - Recent information is clearly more important than older information only in a weighted form.
   - It should be used only after other methods fail.

Historical Assumptions and Limitations

In this chapter we based our initial 1993 projections on historical information using simple extrapolation, combining the percentage growth rate method with the percentage of sales method. We put the greatest emphasis on the percentage growth rate method. Now, let's look at how you can modify this initial projection, understanding the limitations straight extrapolations have on the accuracy of your projections.

Accounting Assumptions

Failing to understand accounting assumptions can lead to extreme errors in financial forecasting. You must clearly understand how the firm's accounting is done, the types of modifications that have been made in accounting over time and the accuracy of the accounting statements.

Changes in Accounting Methods — Changes in accounting methods can cause a great deal of confusion when doing financial statement analysis. For example, if a firm uses the inventory valuation method of "last in, first out" (the inventory is priced based on the first goods coming in being the last goods going out, leaving the oldest goods in inventory), this produces one set of numbers. If a "first in, first out" method is used, the numbers will be different. If the firm changes from one method to another, this can greatly affect the balance sheet and income statements. It makes trying to forecast over a particular period of time considerably more difficult. Another common example is a change in depreciation methods. Any change in accounting methods or the way the firm does business must be understood before a forecaster can proceed with even an initial forecast based on historical assumptions.

Changes in Accounting Periods — Changes in accounting periods can cause substantial differences in the way statements look over a period of time. For example, assume a firm had large sales in December, and the cut-off period was December 20. Then the cut-off date was changed to December 31 because the business included a great deal of Christmas sales. This would seriously distort December sales from one year to the next. This may also be the case if you change your accounting period from year to year.

Changes in Other Accounting Methodology — Any other changes in accounting methods, such as time periods or the way expenses are accounted for may throw the analysis off when evaluating financial ratios or making financial forecasts. Therefore, it is critical when doing financial statement analysis or forecasting to fully understand whether the statements you are looking at are really meaningful. When conducting analyses over time, it becomes more complicated because changing accounting procedures and methodologies causes accounting statements to be different.

Historical Environment

When using past information to forecast the future, it is important to understand the historical environment that existed when the information you are using was created. An understanding of the firm's historical environment is as important to understanding its present and future as it is for a nation or state. A firm will take on a personality or culture of its own formed by its internal and external environment. For example, the firm's management may have been through very difficult times and hence is very conservative in its business decisions. This may account for the low level of debt used by our sample firm.

Past Economic Conditions — Past economic conditions can have a major impact on the numbers you use. For example, growth rates in the economy, different employment levels, interest rates, inflation rates, etc., can have a dramatic impact on the financial statement. If you are dealing with a period when there is dramatic inflation and oil prices are rising rapidly, you might have tremendous increases in expenses that would not serve as an accurate example for predicting future expenses.

Past Conditions of Your Specific Business — Even though you may be familiar with your firm's economic history, it is important to understand how it was affected by economic conditions. Your firm may prosper in economic downturns and suffer when the economy is booming. The historical/financial relationship of your firm to international, national and local economic conditions can be a powerful tool to help you forecast the future.

Living in the Future

Even though we use the past to predict the future, understand that you will be living in the future and do not rely unduly on the past.

> The Past as History — One extreme is to assume that history is not useful. Some analysts say that since so many changing economic conditions caused ups and downs in a firm's financial fortunes over the years, the use of historical information is largely useless. In most cases, this isn't true. A great deal can be learned from history so that a firm doesn't repeat its mistakes, particularly in bad conditions.
>
> The Past as Experience — Most analysts consider using the past as experience and assume that history will project itself somewhat into the future. Use this approach with caution. (Even though historical information is valuable, you realize it must be modified to predict the future.) History is a guide to the future.
>
> Using Year-to-Date Information — Rather than using complete years as you have done, look at year-to-date information as well as annual, historical information. The term year-to-date means using all of the information from the current year even though it may not be a full year.

Forecast Scenarios — What if . . . ?

Often, managers use forecast scenarios or various types of forecasts to look at what will happen if certain conditions exist. Traditionally, forecasts have been done on the basis of the most likely forecast, the best forecast and the worst forecast. Making forecasts in these three categories gives you the opportunity to see what would happen if things go as expected under the most pessimistic circumstances and what would be the most prosperous situation for the firm. Let's take a look at the most likely forecast. To compute a most likely forecast, use Table IV-5.

TABLE IV - 5
Forecast Scenarios

Account	1992	1993 Most Likely Forecasts	Assumptions % Growth Rate	% of Sales Standard	% of Sales Actual
Sales	2,436,000	2,704,000	11.0	100.0	100.0
Cost of Goods Sold:					
Materials	925,500	1,009,700	9.1	38.6	37.3
Labor	584,600	632,500	8.2	24.0	23.4
Heat, Light & Power	87,700	96,500	10.0	3.6	3.6
Indirect Labor	146,200	158,000	8.1	6.2	5.8
Depreciation	53,600	59,000	10.0	2.2	2.2
Gross Margin	638,400	748,300			
Operating Expenses:					
Selling Expenses	243,600	270,200	10.9	10.0	10.0
Admin. Expenses	280,600	303,000	8.0	11.8	11.2
Total Selling & Admin. Expenses	524,200				
Earnings Before Interest & Taxes	114,200	175,100			
Interest Expenses	11,700	12,900	10.0	0.5	0.5
Net Income Before Taxes	102,500	162,200			
Federal Income Taxes (39%)	40,000	63,300			
Net Income	62,500	98,900			

Using Table IV-5 and the sales and expense figures for 1992, the most likely forecast is completed for you. (To make your own computations for the most likely forecast, turn to Appendix 5.)

It would be easy for us to simply plug in percentage growth rates and make some computations for the most likely forecast; however, the purpose of the most likely forecast is to be as accurate as possible. Each program needs to be examined with regard to revenues and expenses.

Let's estimate the most likely forecast for your sales figure. The example lists an 11 percentage growth rate from the original sales of $2,436,000 for 1992. (Remember, round to the nearest $100.)

Rather than take the overall percentage increase for sales, you can look at each of the different areas of sales (or revenue streams) and forecast each based on what you know about the possibilities for growth. Some of your revenue streams will grow very rapidly and some will not. Forecasting this way will indicate what products are increasing in popularity, demand and sales and those that may not be or are being replaced by other products.

At this point you look at each individual item with regard to cost of goods sold and extend it. For example, if you look at the growth in materials expense, you might look at the individual materials and forecast them based on their individual growth rates, then add them together to get the most likely forecast for materials expense.

This procedure can be repeated for each expense item on the income statement. You should break down your forecast into as much detail as possible to understand the individual impacts of growth, revenues and expenses. The less general and more detailed your forecast is, the more accurate it will be. It is very important to take into account projected changes in your method of sales, method of operations, type of products you may be selling, changes in economic conditions, government regulations, etc. This is the time to do this.

Using the historical information and given current conditions, it's time to forecast the future. This is where judgment, experience and a good deal of common sense come into play, in addition to understanding how to use financial statement numbers. One of the most serious errors made in forecasting is to take historical information and simply project it into the future without considering the numerous factors mentioned. Consider how each individual revenue and expense might change given the program changes, economic changes and other factors that might affect your firm. This is a very important step.

Worst-Case Scenario

In the worst-case scenario, you will typically underestimate some of the revenue growth and overestimate some of the cost growth. See Table IV-6 below for an example of a worst-case scenario.

TABLE IV - 6
Forecast Scenarios

Account	1992	1993 Worst-case Forecasts	Assumptions % Growth Rate	% of Sales Standard	% of Sales Actual
Sales	2,436,000	2,630,900	8.0	100.0	100.0
Cost of Goods Sold:					
Materials	925,500	1,018,100	10.0	38.6	38.7
Labor	584,600	637,200	9.0	24.0	24.2
Heat, Light & Power	87,700	96,500	10.0	3.6	3.7
Indirect Labor	146,200	158,300	8.3	6.2	6.2
Depreciation	53,600	59,000	10.0	2.2	2.2
Gross Margin	638,400	661,800			
Operating Expenses:					
Selling Expenses	243,600	270,900	11.2	10.0	10.0
Admin. Expenses	280,600	304,200	8.4	11.8	11.6
Total Selling & Admin. Expenses	524,200				
Earnings Before Interest & Taxes	114,200	86,700			
Interest Expenses	11,700	12,900	10.0	0.5	0.5
Net Income Before Taxes	102,500	73,800			
Federal Income Taxes (39%)	40,000	29,500			
Net Income	62,500	44,300			

Using the percentage growth rates in column four, the worst-case forecast is computed in column three for each item in column one. (To compute your answers, please turn to Appendix 6.) You can see that in your worst-case scenario, net income dropped from $98,900 in the most likely case to $44,300 in the worst case. This is a rather dramatic drop in the net income. You must make some determinations at this point. If you cannot live with this type of net profit, make changes at this point to avoid the worst-case scenario. Often, when worst-case scenarios are computed, it alerts management to the drastic possibilities that may occur if they allow things to slip. This can stimulate management to make many important changes to keep the business viable. Let's now move to the best-case forecast.

Best-Case Scenario

In the best-case scenario, follow the same procedure you used in other forecasts made to this point. Using the 1992 figures, you should make your best-case forecast for 1993, which is shown in Table IV-7. (To compute your answers turn to Appendix 7.)

In the best-case scenario you somewhat reverse what you did in the worst-case scenario. In this case, you attempt to increase your revenue estimates and decrease your expenditures. You can see the very dramatic impact this has on net income. You have gone from a most likely case of $98,900 to a worst-case scenario of $44,300 and now a best-case scenario of $116,800. By enhancing your revenues and trimming costs, you can substantially increase profit. Being able to see these different forecasts and how in the best case they can substantially improve profits, management should be motivated to make the changes necessary, if possible.

TABLE IV - 7
Forecast Scenarios

Account	1992	1993 Best-case Forecasts	Assumptions % Growth Rate	% of Sales Standard	% of Sales Actual
Sales	2,436,000	2,728,300	12.0	100.0	100.0
Cost of Goods Sold:					
Materials	925,500	1,010,600	9.2	38.6	37.0
Labor	584,600	631,400	8.0	24.0	23.1
Heat, Light & Power	87,700	96,500	10.0	3.7	3.5
Indirect Labor	146,200	157,900	8.0	6.2	5.8
Depreciation	53,600	59,000	10.0	2.2	2.2
Gross Margin	638,400	772,900			
Operating Expenses:					
Selling Expenses	243,600	268,000	10.0	10.0	9.8
Admin. Expenses	280,600	300,200	7.0	11.8	11.0
Total Selling & Admin. Expenses	524,200				
Earnings Before Interest & Taxes	114,200	204,700			
Interest Expenses	11,700	12,900	10.0	0.5	0.5
Net Income Before Taxes	102,500	191,800			
Federal Income Taxes (39%)	40,000	75,000			
Net Income	62,500	116,800			

Summary of Financial Forecasting

These are the basics of financial forecasting. By understanding the income statement, the balance sheet and then making forecasts based on historical information, you obtained a most likely forecast based on simple extrapolation of history. In trying to understand the total environment in which you operate and how history affects you, you developed a best-case and a worst-case scenario. At this point, you should have a good understanding of how financial statement forecasting can be used to enhance the strategic planning process. It must be stressed, once again, that this is only part of the puzzle and you must use a great deal of thought, common sense and other information available to do financial forecasting.

TABLE [illegible]

Forecast [illegible]

			Assumptions		
				% of	% of
		Base [illegible]	Growth	Sales	Sales
Account	19[illegible]	[illegible]	Rate	[illegible]	[illegible]
Sales	[illegible]	[illegible]	[illegible]	[illegible]	[illegible]
Cost of Goods					
Materials	[illegible]	[illegible]		[illegible]	[illegible]
Labor	[illegible]	[illegible]	[illegible]	[illegible]	[illegible]
[illegible]					
[illegible]	[illegible]	[illegible]	[illegible]	[illegible]	[illegible]
[illegible]	[illegible]	[illegible]		[illegible]	[illegible]
Depreciation	[illegible]	[illegible]	[illegible]	[illegible]	[illegible]
Gross Margin	[illegible]	[illegible]		[illegible]	
[illegible]					
[illegible]		[illegible]			
[illegible]	[illegible]	[illegible]		[illegible]	[illegible]
Total Selling [illegible]					
[illegible]					
[illegible]					
[illegible]	[illegible]	[illegible]			
Interest Expense	[illegible]	[illegible]	[illegible]	[illegible]	
Net [illegible]					
[illegible]		[illegible]			
[illegible]					
[illegible]	[illegible]	[illegible]			[illegible]
Net Income	[illegible]	[illegible]			[illegible]

Summary of Financial Forecasting

These are the basics of financial forecasting. By understanding the [illegible] statements, the [illegible] and the [illegible] based on [illegible] information, you [illegible] forecasts based on simple extrapolation of [illegible]. In order to understand the total environment in which [illegible] flow [illegible], and develop [illegible] and [illegible]. At this point you should have a good understanding of [illegible] to enter the strategic planning process. [illegible] piece of the puzzle [illegible] information [illegible] financial forecasting.

5

DEVELOPING AND EXECUTING A BUDGET

The next step in financial and overall business planning is to develop budgets — by divisions or by departments — based on the financial forecasting explained in Chapter 4. Most managers think of a budget from the expense side of the net income equation; although, many times expenses are evaluated based on their individual percentage of sales (forecasted sales volume).

Controlling costs is a difficult task for managers of established enterprises, but it is a unique challenge for entrepreneurs who often are so focused on their new products or services that cost control is the last thing on their minds. When you look into the reasons why many businesses fail in their infancies, lack of control systems seems to be a root cause.

THE BUDGET

A budget is a financial tool that allocates revenues and expenses to divisions or departments. The goal of a budget is to obtain a certain amount of net income from a forecasted volume of sales. Without a budget, it is impossible to know whether the company's actual results are going successfully or that they fit into the entity's overall business plan.

Following are some other benefits of a good budget process.

1. A budget allows for coordination of all the departments of a company. For example, if the company forecasts sales of $10 million, the production department must be allocated sufficient funds to produce enough goods to meet such a goal. The same theory must hold true of all departments in the organization.

2. A budget develops a standard by which department managers' performance is measured. In many businesses, "meeting the budget" is the only standard of evaluating managers. For example, the shipping department is budgeted $125,000 to ship $10 million worth of products. The shipping manager knows that to go over his or her allotted amount of funds could be detrimental to his or her overall performance evaluation.

3. A budget to actual report provides a manager or small business owner a starting point for taking action to control costs and to correct practices that are causing cost overruns. For example, if the chief executive officer notices that actual entertainment expenses for the sales department were $8,000 and the budget was $3,500, he or she can take whatever action deemed appropriate. The first step will most likely be to call the sales manager and inquire about the variance — was it necessary? If so, the CEO usually accepts this answer and realizes that a cost savings of $4,500 in another area will be needed to offset this overrun. However, a variance could mean a problem that requires immediate attention, such as a salesperson submitting non-business related expenses on his or her time reports for

reimbursement. If the budget variances are not checked regularly, such a practice could go unnoticed for months and cost the company a lot of money.

HOW TO PREPARE A BUDGET

The budget process begins with the sales forecast since all of business activities must rely on the anticipated level of sales. Once a sales figure has been established, the amount should be given to the head of each budgetary unit (department): the production manager, the sales manager, the marketing manager, etc.

In smaller businesses, the business owner or the accountant figures the entire budget for the various departments and allows those departments to implement a plan to meet the budget. However, in a larger organization, the task is too big for one individual, so the managers of the various departments are responsible for preparing their own budgets to be approved by the upper levels of management. Individual department managers often have more insight into appropriate budgets for their departments. It is obviously very difficult for the controller of a company to predict the various levels of expenditures needed for the shipping department since an accountant usually has no experience in that area.

Most budgets are prepared for the coming fiscal or calendar year of the business and usually on a month-to-month basis. Some companies use a "floating" budget, which means that each department's budget is constantly updated for the next month. (For example, the budget begins as January through December, but once January is over, January of the next year is added.) This process keeps budgeting on the minds of managers for the entire year instead of once a year. Another reason for this method of budgeting is that it is much easier to make changes once a new fact pattern is known.

Specific industries may have other approaches to the budgeting process. For instance, a seasonal business, such as lawn service, may prepare a budget only once for the entire season. Also, certain industries that deal with long-term projects may budget on a contract-by-contract basis in order to determine the profitability of the individual jobs.

Most budgets start out by identifying expense centers for which management wants controls established. Thus departmental budgets are set up for departments such as production, sales, marketing, general and administrative, etc.

Then the individual budget accounts under each of those departments is determined. For example, the production department includes the following:

Salaries
Fringe benefits
Payroll taxes
Materials
Utilities
Repairs & maintenance of equipment

The budget also may be based on the actual chart of accounts of the accounting system, which may be much more detailed. For example, under the general category of materials, there may be 25 separate accounts that can be controlled and budgeted. The amount of detail of a budget depends a lot on the sophistication of the company and the amount of time it has implemented budgets. The more years a company has budgeted its costs, the more detailed the budgets can be if considered necessary. This much detail can also be a weakness, because it is extremely difficult to budget individual items of materials, for example, with any accuracy.

There is a fine line between too little and too much detail for an accurate budget. It takes practice to develop the right budget for a particular business. For instance, if all advertising costs are lumped together in a department's budget, it is difficult to tell whether print media advertising or the additional salary expense of a new graphic artist caused a budget overrun. For ease, though, it is helpful for the budget to mirror general ledger accounts as much as possible so that the budget system can "piggyback" the accounting system.

Here is an example of a typical budget:

Table V-1

Departmental Budget for December 31, 1992

Sales	$2,700,000
Production Costs	1,800,000
Shipping Costs	100,000
Marketing Costs	300,000
General & Administrative	200,000
Net Income	300,000

This summarized budget provides the total funds to be allocated to each of the departments of the organization. Then each of the department managers determines how to spend his or her allocated funds to most efficiently and effectively establish the targeted sales forecast of $2,700,000.

Following is an example of the detailed budget for the general and administrative department:

Table V-2
General & Administrative Budget for December 31, 1992

Personnel Recruiting Expense	$ 40,000
Accounting	60,000
Security	15,000
Supplies	35,000
Office Equipment	20,000
Interest Expense	30,000
Total General & Administrative Expenses	200,000

SIGNIFICANT FACTS TO REMEMBER ABOUT THE BUDGET

1. The budgeting process takes a lot of practice. Once implemented and used properly, it is a very valuable tool to control costs and increase profitability of a company.

2. Budgets can be as detailed or as summarized as management sees fit as long as they are still useful, especially to the individual with the overall budget responsibilities. Does the budget give the owner or CEO of the company all the information necessary to analyze the progress of the entire business as well as the individual departments?

3. A budget process must continuously be updated for changes in the company's business environment. An outdated budget does not provide useful information. This is a big advantage for the "floating" budget process, which requires budgeters to constantly update it for changing market conditions such as increased prices for raw materials or cutbacks in the sales force as the year progresses.

6

FUNDING FOR GROWTH

Among the ratios previously discussed was the total asset turnover which related a level of sales to the firm's total assets. Norms were established for this as well as other ratios. To stay within the normal relationship of sales to assets, assets must increase to support the increased level of sales. As you saw at the outset, assets equal liabilities plus owners' equity; thus, if assets increase, so must the financing either from funds generated internally through the firm's earnings or by obtaining funds from external sources.

Internal Sources

Internal sources of funds come from the firm's operations. Hopefully the firm can generate enough revenues to cover its expenses and provide funds needed for expansion of assets to support increases in sales and expenses. You cannot automatically assume that if sales and profits are growing you will have enough funding to support continued growth.

Internal sources of funding do not come from what we typically refer to as retained earnings, but instead generate retained earnings. Retained earnings are shown on the balance sheet in the equity section. (This isn't shown on the income statement in this handbook in an effort to keep this as simple as possible.) Retained earnings are part of owners' equity and simply indicate what earnings are being retained to support the asset growth. Retained earnings does not mean that the funds are kept in a particular cash balance and that they are available. It means they are distributed throughout the firm's assets. As the firm retains earnings, it does so by building up inventories and investing in other current and fixed assets. This increase in the asset structure supports the growth of sales. If management control is inadequate, it is possible for one asset to increase too much and create financial difficulty.

Looking at the analysis of the financial statements, you can quickly recall the difficulties the firm was facing. A major difficulty appeared to be very large inventory holdings. Even without a growth in sales this will hamper the firm's operations and may require additional funds beyond what can be generated internally.

External Sources

It may be necessary to turn to external sources of funding such as short-term borrowing, increasing accounts payable, longer-term borrowing from financial institutions or bonds or stock.

You can compute the external fund requirements necessary to support the growth you have had in sales. Following is a formula for estimating these external fund requirements.

$$\text{External Fund Requirements} =$$

$$\left[\left(\frac{\text{Current Assets}}{\text{Sales}} - \frac{\text{Current Liabilities Excluding Notes Payable}}{\text{Sales}}\right) \times \text{The Dollar Change in Sales}\right]$$

MINUS

$$\text{Profit Margin} > \begin{array}{c}\text{New Level}\\ \text{of Sales}\end{array} > \left(1 - \begin{array}{c}\text{Dividend}\\ \text{Payout Ratio}\end{array}\right)$$

or

$$\left[\left(\frac{A}{S} - \frac{L}{S}\right) > S_c\right] - \left[P > S_n > \left(1 - D\right)\right]$$

A = Assets that vary with sales (assumed to be current assets only)
L = Liabilities that vary with sales (current liabilities only excluding notes payable)
S = Current sales
S_c = Change in sales
P = Profit margin
S_n = New level of sales
D = Dividend pay-out ratio

You are attempting to look at what happens when you make the necessary increases in assets and liabilities given a change in sales, knowing what your profit margin and your new level of sales are and what you will pay out in dividends to your shareholders. This formula attempts to see what the net impact of a change in sales will be, given an increase in assets and liabilities and based on how profitable you are minus what you will be paying out to the owners. If there is enough left over for funding requirements internally, you will not need external funds. However, if you do need external funds, you can get an estimate from this computation.

In this case, each variable is given starting from the 1992 statements and using the most-likely forecast given in Chapter 4.

A = \$1,169,300[1]

L = \$243,600 (accounts payable 146,200 + other current liabilities 97,400)[2]

S = \$2,436,000 (1992 sales level)

S_c = \$268,000 (assume an 11 percent change in sales which is the most likely case increase up to 1993)

P = 0.026641 (1992 net income of \$62,500 / 1992 sales of \$2,436,000)

S_n = \$2,704,000 (1993 sales from most likely forecast)

D = 0 (assume no dividends are paid out)

$$\frac{A}{S} = \frac{\$1,169,300}{\$2,436,000} = 0.48$$

$$\frac{L}{S} = \frac{\$243,600}{\$2,436,000} = 0.48$$

$$\left[\left(\frac{A}{S} - \frac{L}{S}\right) > S_c\right] - \left[P > S_n > \left(1 - D\right)\right]$$

.048 – 0.10 x \$268,000 – [0.026 x \$2,704,000 x (1 – 0)]
= \$101,840 - \$70,304
= \$ 31,536 of external funds required

[1] *It is assumed that only current assets will vary with an increase in sales of this magnitude. Fixed assets (plant and equipment) are assumed to remain the same in the short-run.*

[2] *It is assumed that notes payable will not increase with sales without active outside borrowing by management. This is what you are trying to determine, so it is not included in internal funds generated.*

This is only a rough estimate of the external funding requirements for the firm. Sources of funds other than those shown may generate cash flow. For example, depreciation is not a cash expense in the current period. In determining the amount of funds generated internally this period, depreciation may be omitted from the expense. If we took this into account, we would not have to seek external funds.

As we discussed earlier, the inventory turnover was much too slow. In other words, the inventory is too large relative to sales. Consider the impact of the reduction of inventory on external funding requirements. Assume all variables stay the same in our previous example except for the level of variable assets needed relative to sales. The inventory for 1992 is $730,800 with an inventory turnover of 3.33 times. If this turnover were increased to 9.8 times (the industry standard), this would mean an inventory level of $248,600, i.e. sales of ($2,436,000 / 9.8). The impact of this on fund usage is dramatic as you can see when recomputing the assets that change with sales and external funding. First, look at assets that change with sales.

	With Current Levels of Inventory	**With Inventory Level Reduced By Increasing Turnover to 9.8**
Cash	$ 194,900	$194,900
Receivables	243,600	243,600
Inventory	730,800	248,600
	$1,169,300	$687,100

Recomputing the assets that change as a percentage of sales:

$$\frac{A}{S} = \frac{\$687,100}{\$2,436,000} = 0.28$$

External funding requirements if inventory were lower:

[(0.28 – 0.10) › $243,600] – [0.026 › 2,704,000 › 1]

$43,848 – $70,304

= – $26,456 (excess funding)

Assuming all assets except inventory maintain their proper relationships to sales and inventory is reduced to an appropriate size, you now have no external funding needs. In fact, you have generated an extra $26,456 to use in operations. This makes a significant difference of $57,992 — a change from needing $31,536 to having $26,456 in excess financing. Through more efficient use of assets, the total size (and financing needs) of the firm may be reduced.

Key Points: Funding for Growth

1. Carefully analyze assets to ensure that each is necessary.

2. Ensure that each asset is being utilized as effectively and efficiently as possible.

3. Review liabilities to estimate their proper size relative to the firm's assets and sales.

4. Utilize liabilities that naturally arise in the normal course of business (accounts payable) to fund some of the growth.

5. Remember that fixed assets (plant and equipment) may not need to be expanded for growth in the short run, but may become an important consideration in the long term.

6. Plan ahead for funding growth needs by utilizing forecasts and estimating funding requirements for them.

APPENDIX

APPENDIX 1

Computation of Financial Ratios

Ratio	Method of Computation	Computation	Result
Current	Current Assets / Current Liabilities	1,169,300 / 438,500	2.67
Acid Test	Current Assets – Inventory / Current Liabilities	438,500 / 438,500	1
Avg. Collection Period	Accounts Receivable / Annual Credit Sales / 360	243,600 / 2,436,000/360	36 days
Acc. Rec. Turnover	Credit Sales / Avg. Accounts Receivable	2,436,00 / 243,600	10 x
Inventory Turnover	Sales / Average Inventory	2,436,000 / 730,800	3.33%
Fixed Asset Turnover	Sales / Fixed Assets	2,436,000 / 535,900	4.55%
Total Asset Turnover	Sales / Total Assets	2,436,000 / 1,705,200	1.43%
Debt to Equity	Debt / Equity	633,400 / 1,071,800	59.1%
Debt to Total Assets	Debt / Total Assets	633,400 / 1,705,200	37.1%
Times Interest Earned	Earnings Before Int. & Taxes / Interest Payment	114,200 / 11,700	9.76%
Gross Profit Margin	Gross Profit / Sales	638,400 / 2,436,000	26.2%
Net Profit Margin	Net Profit / Sales	62,500 / 2,436,000	2.57%
Return on Assets (ROA)	Net Profit / Assets	62,500 / 1,705,200	3.67%
Return on Equity	Net Profits / Equity	62,500 / 1,071,800	5.83%

* The ratio is multiplied by 100 to put it in percentage form.

APPENDIX 2

Growth Rates (in %)

	88-89	89-90	90-91	91-92	Average	Projection
Sales	10	10	9.24	9.75	9.75	
Cost of Goods Sold:						
Materials	10			9		
Labor		7		9		
Heat, Light & Power		9	10	11	9.75	
Indirect Labor	6	9				
Depreciation		10	10	10	10	
Selling Expenses	11	10		12	10.75	
Administrative Expenses	8	9		8	8.25	
Interest Expenses	10	10	10	10	10	

APPENDIX 3

Percent of Sales Forecasts

	1988	1989	1990	1991	1992	Avg.	Proj.
Sales	100	100	100	100	100	100	
Cost of Goods Sold:							
Materials	39.1	39.1	38.3	38.3	38.0	38.6	
Labor	25.4	25.1	24.4	24.1	24.0	24.6	
Heat, Light & Power	3.6	3.6	3.5	3.6	3.6	3.6	
Indirect Labor	6.5	6.2	6.2	6.2	6.0	6.2	
Depreciation	2.2	2.2	2.2	2.2	2.2	2.2	
Selling Expenses	9.6	9.7	9.7	9.8	10.0	9.8	
Administrative Expenses	12.2	12.0	11.9	11.7	11.5	11.8	
Interest Expenses	0.5	0.5	0.5	0.5	0.5	0.5	

APPENDIX 4

Preliminary Forecasts

Account	1992	1993 Preliminary Forecasts	Assumptions % Growth Rate	% of Sales Standard	% of Sales Actual
Sales	2,436,000		10%	100	
Cost of Goods Sold:					
Materials	925,500		9.0	38.6	
Labor	584,600		8.5	24.0	
Heat, Light & Power	87,700		10.0	3.6	
Indirect Labor	146,200		8.0	6.2	
Depreciation	53,600		10.0	2.2	
Gross Margin	638,400				
Operating Expenses:					
Selling Expenses	243,600		11.0	10.0	
Admin. Expenses	280,600		8.0	11.8	
Total Selling & Admin. Expenses	524,200				
Earnings Before Interest & Taxes	114,200				
Interest Expenses	11,700		10.0	.5	
Net Income Before Taxes	102,500				
Federal Income Taxes (39%)	40,000				
Net Income	62,500				

APPENDIX 5

Forecast Scenarios

Account	1992	1993 Most Likely Forecasts	Assumptions % Growth Rate	% of Sales Standard	% of Sales Actual
Sales	2,436,000		11.0	100.0	
Cost of Goods Sold:					
Materials	925,500		9.1	38.6	
Labor	584,600		8.2	24.0	
Heat, Light & Power	87,700		10.0	3.6	
Indirect Labor	146,200		8.1	6.2	
Depreciation	53,600		10.0	2.2	
Gross Margin	638,400				
Operating Expenses:					
Selling Expenses	243,600		10.9	10.0	
Admin. Expenses	280,600		8.0	11.8	
Total Selling & Admin. Expenses	524,200				
Earnings Before Interest & Taxes	114,200				
Interest Expenses	11,700		10.0	0.5	
Net Income Before Taxes	102,500				
Federal Income Taxes (39%)	40,000				
Net Income	62,500				

APPENDIX 6

Forecast Scenarios

Account	1992	1993 Worst-case Forecasts	Assumptions % Growth Rate	% of Sales Standard	% of Sales Actual
Sales	2,436,000		100.0	100.0	
Cost of Goods Sold:					
Materials	925,500		10.0	38.6	
Labor	584,600		9.0	24.0	
Heat, Light & Power	87,700		10.0	3.6	
Indirect Labor	146,200		8.3	6.2	
Depreciation	53,600		10.0	2.2	
Gross Margin	638,400				
Operating Expenses:					
Selling Expenses	243,600		11.2	10.0	
Admin. Expenses	280,600		8.4	11.8	
Total Selling & Admin. Expenses	524,200				
Earnings Before Interest & Taxes	114,200				
Interest Expenses	11,700		10.0	0.5	
Net Income Before Taxes	102,500				
Federal Income Taxes (39%)	40,000				
Net Income	62,500				

APPENDIX 7
Forecast Scenarios

			Assumptions		
Account	1992	1993 Best-case Forecasts	% Growth Rate	% of Sales Standard	% of Sales Actual
Sales	2,436,000		12.0	100.0	
Cost of Goods Sold:					
Materials	925,500		9.2	38.6	
Labor	584,600		8.0	24.0	
Heat, Light & Power	87,700		10.0	3.7	
Indirect Labor	146,200		8.0	6.2	
Depreciation	53,600		10.0	2.2	
Gross Margin	638,400				
Operating Expenses:					
Selling Expenses	243,600		10.0	10.0	
Admin. Expenses	280,600		7.0	11.8	
Total Selling & Admin. Expenses	524,200				
Earnings Before Interest & Taxes	114,200				
Interest Expenses	11,700		10.0	0.5	
Net Income Before Taxes	102,500				
Federal Income Taxes (39%)	40,000				
Net Income	62,500				

GLOSSARY OF TERMS

Accounts Payable: Goods, services and supplies purchased for use in business operations that have not yet been paid for.

Accounts Receivable Turnover: Computed by taking annual credit sales only divided by average accounts receivable. Provides information about how efficiently accounts receivable is being managed.

$$\text{Account Receivable Turnover} = \frac{\text{Annual Credit Sale}}{\text{Average Accounts Receivable}}$$

Accrual Accounting: An accounting method that attempts to match the expenses incurred by the firm with the revenue generated in a particular time period.

Acid-Test Ratio: A measure of the firm's ability to pay its liabilities using assets that are cash or only one step away from cash. It is calculated by subtracting inventory from the current assets, then dividing by the current liabilities.

$$\text{Acid-Test Ratio} = \frac{\text{Current Assets} - \text{Inventory}}{\text{Current Liabilities}}$$

Activity Ratios: Used to determine how effective the firm is in utilizing its assets in the management of the firm. These ratios are often referred to as asset utilization ratios or turnover ratios.

Assets: All economic resources owned or controlled by the firm that are expected to provide future benefits for the firm.

Asset Utilization Ratios: Also known as activity or turnover ratios. Used to determine how effective the firm is in utilizing its assets in the management of the firm.

Average Collection Period: An important measure in determining how well accounts receivable is being managed. Computed by dividing average accounts receivable by annual credit sales, which have been divided by 360.

$$\text{Average Collection Period} = \frac{\text{Account Receivable}}{\text{Annual Credit Sales / 360}}$$

Bonds: Long-term debt issued by a firm. The firm agrees to pay the holder the face value at a maturity date and make periodic interest payments at a rate specified on the bond. Usually used to help finance current operations and new acquisitions of property, plant or equipment.

Cash Flow: The cash that comes in (cash inflow) or goes out (cash outflow) of a business.

Claims on Assets: The right of creditors, preferred stockholders and owners to the assets of the firm. Claims to assets of the firm first go to creditors, followed by preferred stockholders and lastly to the common stockholders.

Common Equity: Claims against the assets of a business by its owners. It represents the owners' investment in the firm's assets.

Common-Size Analysis: Attempts to take the dollar size factor out of comparing financial information by using percentages to indicate the relative size of individual items relative to the total, usually total assets on the balance sheet and revenue on the income statement.

Convertible Bonds: Bonds that may, under certain conditions, be converted into common stock.

Current Ratio: The ratio of the current assets to current liabilities. Gives some indication of the firm's ability to pay its current liabilities. Computed by dividing current assets by current liabilities.

Debenture Bonds: Bonds not secured by specific assets of the firm.

Debt to Net Worth Ratio (Debt to Stockholders' Equity): Measures the amount of total debt relative to the stockholders' investment.

$$\text{Debt to Stockholders' Equity} = \frac{\text{Total Debt}}{\text{Stockholder's Equity}}$$

Debt to Total Assets Ratio: Computed by dividing total debt by total assets. Reveals the proportion of total assets financed by total debt.

$$\text{Debt to Total Assests Ratio} = \frac{\text{Total Debt}}{\text{Total Assets}}$$

Equity: Represents the sum of common stock, preferred stock, additional paid-in capital, retained earnings and treasury stock.

Financial Ratio Analysis: Analysis used to measure a firm's financial strengths and weaknesses.

Fixed Assets (Net Fixed Assets): Buildings, machinery and vehicles used to generate revenue for the business, which are not for sale in the normal course of business activity. Also described as "property, plant and equipment." Net fixed assets is fixed assets minus their accumulated depreciation.

Fixed Asset Turnover Ratio: Measures how well the firm is generating sales from its fixed assets. Computed by dividing sales by fixed assets.

$$\text{Fixed Asset Turnover Ratio} = \frac{\text{Sales}}{\text{Fixed Assets}}$$

Fixed Charge Coverage Ratio: Shows how able the firm is to meet fixed charges such as interest payments, leases and possibly even sinking fund payments for debt. It is computed by dividing the income available for meeting fixed charges by the fixed charges.

$$\text{Fixed Charge Coverage} = \frac{\text{Income Available for Fixed Charges}}{\text{Fixed Charges}}$$

Gross Profit Margin Ratio: Computed by dividing sales minus cost of goods sold by total sales. Gives some idea of how sales and cost of goods sold are being managed relative to sales.

$$\text{Gross Profit Margin Ratio} = \frac{\text{Sales} - \text{Cost of Goods Sold}}{\text{Total Sales}}$$

Indenture: The agreement between a firm's bondholders and stockholders, which includes all of the features and restrictive covenants.

Individual Current Asset Ratio: Determines the relationship of each individual current asset to total current liabilities. It is computed by dividing each current asset by total liabilities.

$$\text{Individual Current Asset Ratio} = \frac{\text{Each Individual Current Asset}}{\text{Total Liabilities}}$$

Inventory Turnover Ratio: Calculated by either dividing sales or cost of goods sold by the firm's average inventory. Gives a general idea of whether a firm is carrying too large an inventory relative to sales.

$$\text{Inventory Turnover Ratio} = \frac{\text{Sales}}{\text{Average Inventory}}$$

Liabilities: The economic obligations (debts) of the firm, both short- and long-term. Examples are payables, bonds and mortgages.

Net Profit Margin Ratio: Net profit (can be before or after taxes) divided by sales. Critical in evaluating how well a firm is doing.

$$\text{Net Profit Margin} = \frac{\text{Net Profit}}{\text{Sales}}$$

Notes Payable: Short-term obligations, possibly to a bank or other financial institution, that are payable in one year or less.

Par Value: The stated value per share printed on the face of common or preferred stock.

Quick-Test Ratio: Another name for acid-test ratio. A measure of the firm's ability to pay its liabilities using assets that are cash or only one step away from cash. It is calculated by subtracting inventory from the current assets then dividing by the current liabilities.

$$\text{Quick Test} = \frac{\text{Current Assets} - \text{Inventory}}{\text{Current Liabilities}}$$

Receivables: Amounts that are due to the firm in less than one year.

Return on Total-Assets Ratio: Measures the return on total assets the firm has made (ROA) and is computed by dividing the net profit by total assets. The ratio indicates whether a firm is effectively using its total assets to generate profit.

$$\text{Return on Total Assets} = \frac{\text{Net Profit}}{\text{Total Assets}}$$

Return on Net-Worth Ratio (Return on Stockholders' Equity): Indicates what kind of profit the firm has generated on owners' equity. It is computed by dividing net profit by stockholders' equity.

$$\text{Return of Net Worth Ratio} = \frac{\text{Net Profit}}{\text{Stockholders' Equity}}$$

Revenues: Amounts charged to a firm's customers for goods and services received during a particular accounting period.

Sinking Fund Payments: Payments made by a firm into an account to be used in retiring a portion of bonds each year.

Subordinated Debenture: Debenture bonds that are secondary in their claim on the firm's assets and income to other bonds.

Times Interest Earned Ratio: Indicates if interest charges are covered by earnings before interest and taxes. Computed by dividing earnings before interest and taxes by interest charges.

$$\text{Times Interest Earned Ratio} = \frac{\text{Earnings Before Interest \& Taxes}}{\text{Interest Charges}}$$

Total-Asset Turnover: Indicates the amount of sales being generated from the firm's total assets. The ratio is computed by dividing sales by total assets.

$$\text{Total Asset Turnover Ratio} = \frac{\text{Sales}}{\text{Total Assets}}$$

Turnover Ratios: Also referred to as asset utilization or activity ratios. Used to determine how effective the firm is in utilizing its assets in the management of the firm.

[illegible]

[illegible]

[illegible]

[illegible]

[illegible]

[illegible]

INDEX